MOSQUITOS

A NOVEL BY MICHAEL COLE

SEVEREDPRESS

MOSQUITOS

Copyright © 2023 MICHAEL COLE

WWW.SEVEREDPRESS.COM

ISBN: 978-1-922861-68-9

CHAPTER 1

Following the glass window shattering came a rush of warm, humid air. A droning sound filled the computer room. Panicked cries and sounds of struggle added to the chaos, concluding with the thud of Dr. Martin Geyer being forced to the floor. He screamed as a sharp instrument penetrated his lower abdomen. Next came a series of coughs and gags, as though he was getting waterboarded.

Dr. William Aaron was at the door with Dr. Susan Cabot when he looked back. He saw his friend and colleague on his back just in time to witness his normally brown skin and hair turn pasty white. The eyes shrunk into the sockets, his dry, wrinkly cheeks suctioning between his teeth. His neck, which he used to complain was a little too fat, was now hugging the spinal vertebrae.

Above him was a mass of wings fluttering over an inflating abdomen.

"Go. GO!" William forced Susan out the door. At first, he thought the bugs would not get inside the compound. The sound of shattering windows upstairs and in the back rooms proved him wrong. They were determined, persistent, and strong enough to force their way inside.

The two scientists retreated into the main lobby, just in time to see another one of their associates get overwhelmed. It was Jake Wells, the electrician. He slashed with his screwdriver as though it was a machete. His attackers attacked with their own weapons. In

1

addition to their stake-like mouths, they were gifted with six long legs. Normal-sized specimens never made great use of their appendages other than for walking. These giants, however, quickly learned they could use them for slashing and pinning, which was exactly what these two did to Jake.

One of the razor-tipped feet caught him on the left cheek, flaying it open, exposing muscle tissue and teeth. Jake spun on his boots, a flab of cheek dangling from his jawline. The bleeding would not last long. The second attacker plowed into him like a hawk swooping down to seize a critter. Instead of taking to the sky with its catch, the creature pinned him to the floor. Jake's fingers clawed against the carpet, rearing his head back in agony. Both bugs rammed their proboscises into his flesh and began to suction every drop of fluid.

In a matter of seconds, Jake transformed from a thirty-nine-year-old, slightly overweight tradesman from Arizona to a dry, ghoulish shell.

"Oh, my god," Susan said. She and William looked beyond the stiffened electrician to the broken window. On the other side, more thirsty insects began to gather, emboldened by the breach in their preys' supposed safe haven. In about five seconds, they would fill the lobby.

William goaded her back into the hallway. They ran to the north side of the facility, near storage.

"Wait!" Susan said, slowing down. "I think I hear more down this way…"

"Keep going," William said. He was impressed with his ability to keep himself calm and collected, even if just barely. The shock of the current reality was potent, fueled by the abrupt nature of how it occurred.

The day had started off like any other. Routine tests in the morning, disposal of failed projects in the northwest canal, blood draws of the current specimens. A few minutes after nine, Paul Letter, the vet tech on site, reported hearing strange buzzing sounds to the south. Nobody thought much of it. Then at ten, he heard it again. A few minutes after that, the attack commenced. Like demons descending from Heaven, of all places, they swarmed the camp. Nothing was spared. Humans, livestock, test subjects… everything with blood flowing through its veins was targeted.

As they approached storage, they could hear someone screaming outside. More alarming was the sound of buzzing wings straight ahead. There were bugs inside the north end of the compound.

Susan slowed and put her hand out to stop William. "Doctor, they're near storage..."

"Keep going," he said.

"But Doctor…"

"Keep going! That's the only place to hide. If you don't get down there, you'll die!"

Against her instinct, Susan ran *toward* the sound of buzzing wings. They crashed through a set of double doors. Sure enough, there were at least five insects inside. Three of them were on the floor, siphoning fluid from the bodies of two maintenance men.

Susan put a hand to her mouth. Self-preservation was stalled by shock. Despite their shrunken appearance, she recognized both men. One was Trent Powell, the custodian. The black tattoo on his left forearm had been fading over the years. Now, compared to the dry, pasty flesh, it stood out as though brand new, though its shape was unrecognizable due to the withered skin. The other victim was Mike Helm, the groundskeeper. His long, dark hair was now thin and stringy, barely attached to his tightening scalp. His glasses had fallen off, exposing open sockets which originally contained his bright blue eyes. Now, there was just a soggy greenish-white substance in there.

The other two bugs were perched on the back wall near the ceiling. They shook their wings, ready to attack the new arrivals.

William led Susan to the right. Fifteen feet ahead was a thick oak door which led to the cellar.

Don't be locked. Don't be locked... he turned the handle. "Oh, thank God." He opened the cellar door and pushed Susan inside. She went down the first few steps and looked up at him.

"William, come on!"

"No. I gotta get to the radio room. If we don't get a message out, we'll be trapped here for weeks before someone comes." There was no time to argue. He slammed the door shut and spun on his heels to go back the way he came. Immediately, he had to duck to avoid an oncoming flyer. It zipped over his body, the buzzing of its wings sounding like saw blades in the air.

William sprinted as fast as he could, slamming the double doors behind him. He was confident Susan would be fine, as long as she remained in the cellar. There was food and water down there, enough to last her a good while. The door was thick. The dumb bugs were persistent, but so far, it appeared they only attempted to break through windows. They were fierce, but not intelligent. William believed they only broke through windows because they could see through them. Susan just needed to be quiet. If she made a commotion down there, they would hear her and possibly try chipping away at the door. Otherwise, William predicted they would forget she was even down there and move on— though only after killing all other prey in the area.

He turned left at the next juncture and took a flight of stairs to the second floor. There, he went through another hallway, which contained private offices. Three doors ahead on the left was the radio room. The door was ajar and a vile smell radiated from within.

William pushed the door open and stepped inside. On the floor was Janet Baily, the communications officer. She was hardly recognizable. Her jaw was hyper-extended, the fillings in her crowns in full view. Her tongue was thin and lizard-like, drained of fluid like the rest of her body.

It took a moment for William to overcome the urge to break down and panic. That inner calm was just about gone now. He forced himself to think logically.

Like what you told Susan: get a distress call out, or else it will take weeks or even months for someone to come. In that event, death is certain.

He took a seat in the operator chair. In previous months, he had stood over Janet's shoulder while they communicated with the company station in Georgia. In doing so, he got a good sense of how the equipment worked.

William twisted the knob to the Georgia Station's channel and pressed the transmitter

"This is Doctor William Aaron. We require immediate extraction. The compound has been breached. We have multiple fatalities. Please send help. We're under attack by…"

The ray of sunshine streaming through the window was suddenly obscured by a large, winged figure. As William stood up to run, it zipped through the already broken glass. He saw a flutter of wings and the flailing of legs, which mercilessly tore at his lab coat and dress shirt.

Not only was the bug monstrous in size, but in strength as well. It easily overpowered him, using its frenzied method of attack to drive William on his back. He smacked its slimy, rigid head with his hands, but it did no good. The bony, pointed-tipped proboscis emerged, dripping slime.

He yelled out, then convulsed as the barb plunged into his stomach. There was overwhelming pain, followed by a weird sense of having his insides vacuumed out. All of a sudden, he felt severely dehydrated, then lightheaded. The last few seconds of life were spent numb while every last drop of blood was transferred into the insect's abdomen.

The bug took flight, leaving William's dry, bony corpse on the carpet. His remains, like the other bodies that filled the compound, would serve as food for the normal-sized insects that would eventually come through the broken windows.

CHAPTER 2

"This is Doctor William Aaron. We require immediate extraction. The compound has been breached. We have multiple fatalities. Please send help. We're under attack by..."

Dr. Liz Moore clicked the mouse, ending the flood of static that followed the transmission. Dabbing her sweaty forehead with a tablecloth, she turned to the three large screens mounted on the wall. It was the only first-world tech in this wooden shack that served as both her quarters and office. A billion-dollar company, and yet they were too cheap to build lodgings suitable for a woman of her stature.

On the center screen was Jed Pervis, the president of Lexington Corp. He was a handsome man in his mid-thirties, the successor to his father, the founder of the company. On the righthand screen was Vice President Claire Fairview. She was a young, polite type, a smokescreen of her true, vile nature. On the left monitor was Mel Navarone, who was the most stereotypical in appearance. He was balding, had some neck fat squeezing over his shirt collar, and had no vision outside of the almighty dollar.

As usual, he was the first to speak.

"What do you think occurred?"

"I don't know. I wasn't there," Liz replied. "You heard the same transmission I did. We can only speculate."

"Dr. Moore, you are more connected with the details of this project than any of us," Jed Pervis said. "Clearly, you must have some insight."

Liz felt a new tremor in her hand. It always started in the hand. Today, it was starting a little earlier than usual. It was probably the stress of being grilled by the suits that kicked it off. Her fix would have to wait. Not that the suits would take her off the assignment if they knew—hardly anyone in this company was clean—but if they knew, it would give them ammunition should they decide to pin something on her. News reporters were always looking into the company's activities. Should the details of their research get released to the public, Jed Pervis had no shortage of scapegoats. It was a matter of who was most likely to get the axe. Even someone with Liz Moore's skillsets was not invulnerable.

To quell the shakes, she went with her over-the-counter fixation: Peppermint altoids. She dug the container from her pocket and tossed a couple of candies into her mouth.

"In the past few years, there have been new reports of bandits gathering in the Congo area," she said. "That's just one guess. It's a wild place. For all I know, they've been attacked by wild animals."

"What about the test subjects?" Jed Pervis asked.

"The rats? Doubtful they would be able to do something like this," Liz said.

Vice President Claire Fairview grinned disparagingly. "I'm sorry. Rats?"

Liz tossed another altoid into her mouth, preventing herself from saying something too unruly to the woman with great legs, exposed cleavage, and no brain.

"We test with rats, yes. This project is designed to test medication, is it not?"

Clare had a bemused smirk on her face. "Well, yes, but... *that* big? You guys are talking as though the rats overran the research facility."

"My people have produced an effective serum," Liz said. She leaned over her desktop computer and brought up some photo images sent by the lab. One image showed a typical white rat standing next to one of the scientists. Clare began fidgeting with some of her shoulder-length hair, put off by the fact that the specimen was as large as a husky.

"Oh…"

"Has there been any contact with the dock facility?" Mel Navarone asked.

"No," Liz said. "I've made numerous attempts to call. Nobody's even picking up the satellite phone."

Mel pursed his lips. "I don't like this. Mr. Pervis, is it possible that this could be the result of sabotage? It would not be the first time a rival company attempted to seize control of our work."

"I don't know," Jed said. "I've never seen any go to this extent. However, the developments we've made in that facility are too valuable."

Liz shut her eyes, tightening her fists behind her back. *You mean MY developments. You haven't done shit except sit in an air-conditioned office.*

"Warlords are most likely," Jed Pervis continued. "That compound is full of valuable supplies. Medication, technology, fuel."

"Perhaps we should send in a rescue team," Clare said. "Do we have contracts with the military?"

Liz could not contain her smirk. *How'd this bitch get this high up in the company? Eh, like I don't know the answer…*

"No, we have private contractors," Jed said.

"Samuel Ziler?" Mel said.

"Correct. I'll get in touch with him as soon as we end this conference," Jed said. "Dr. Moore?"

"Yes?"

"How rusty is your Army training?"

Liz felt a rush of blood causing a heightened state of alert. "My Army training? Like riding a bike, sir."

"Good," Jed said. "Because you're going in with the team. You're the only one who can access the computer system. If indeed something has happened there, I want you to download all data from the computers. The scientists there have made significant progress and we cannot risk losing that data."

"You got it."

Another altoid was crunched between her teeth.

This conference needed to end because the adrenaline was sparking the need for a significant fix. It had been years since she had been on any kind of combat deployment.

"Sir, when should I expect the team?"

"They'll be on their way five minutes after this conversation. Expect them by tomorrow."

"And if they're busy on another assignment?"

Jed chuckled. "Trust me. The amount I'll pay, they'll drop whatever task they're on and come straight over. Expect their arrival by tomorrow morning."

And just like that, the conference came to a close. The screens went black, leaving Liz in silence. On the other side of the Atlantic, Jed Pervis was getting in touch with Samuel Ziler and his band of mercenaries.

"Great. Just great."

The shakes were getting bad.

Liz marched to the back of the room and unlocked the drawer where she kept her stash.

CHAPTER 3

For Samuel Ziler, it never seemed there was time to relax. Eighteen months ago, he had spent over a million dollars on his thirty-acre ranch in Kansas, yet he only spent a total of thirty-eight days living in it. There was always a government agency or a private company that needed some dirty work done off the books. Such entities only hired the best, and Ziler's team was the *best* of the best.

Thirty-six hours ago, he returned home after a two-month tour, tracking pirates in Burma, which then led to two rescue missions in Indonesia. Human trafficking was as notorious there as it was anywhere else. No matter what corner of the earth Ziler visited, there was always evil. And sometimes, he worked for evil. Thus, he learned the moral cost of living the life of a mercenary. Soldiers fought for honor and brotherhood, even if their military and political commanders did not. Mercenaries worked for the almighty dollar, and only the most unpleasant jobs paid the best.

Ziler was seated on his front porch when his phone rang. At face value, he looked like an average red-blooded American. He had a thin, brown beard covering the scars of war that permanently marked his jawline. He wore glasses when he read, had cowboy boots on his feet, and was dressed in dirty jeans and a plaid shirt.

Only the people who knew him saw the killing machine that gently rocked on that chair. Jed Pervis was one of those people.

Ziler brought the phone to his ear. "Yeah?"

"Captain Samuel Ziler. I suppose you know who this is."

"Jed Pervis. I know you all too well."

"Am I catching you at a bad time?"

Ziler snorted. "Like you'd care."

Jed laughed. *"Yeah, you do know me all too well. I'll get right to the point. I have an assignment for you. I'm willing to provide transport at any rendezvous location you select. The payment is two million."*

Ziler looked at his field, which he had spent most of yesterday mowing. *So much for enjoying a little peace and quiet.*

"What's the assignment? Rescue? Assassination? Sabotage? All of the above?"

Jed chuckled. This was perhaps the only occasion where he would not staunchly deny that such practices were employed in the world of pharmaceuticals.

"Well, Captain, it's a little complicated. It's more of an escort."

The incessant use of his rank during his U.S. Marine Corps service was grating. When his men used it, it was genuinely out of habit or genuine respect, for most of them knew him while he was on active duty. Men like Jed Pervis, on the other hand, used it as a pathetic means of pandering. In their minds, they believed they were kissing up to the egos of veterans. Perhaps it worked for others. All Ziler knew was he personally did not care for it. Especially now, given the details of the assignment.

"I'm babysitting someone?"

"It's not that bad. She has military training herself, and she knows exactly what she's looking for. To elaborate, we have a laboratory in the Congo Jungle. The specifics will be explained during your briefing in Cameroon, but for the sake of convenience, I'll keep it short and simple. The purpose of the laboratory is to

develop new vaccines from a new flower we've discovered there."

"You're asking me to escort one of your people to your own lab?" Ziler said. "Let me guess: communications went dark."

"It's been over a week, and we have received zero contact. They have repairmen on site with plenty of equipment for radio repair and replacement. I'm not inclined to believe it's a communications issue. Not to mention, a distress call was placed right before the lab went dark."

Right away, Ziler's mind began pondering the various possibilities. The first was violent animal life, but that seemed unlikely. Jed Pervis would not station a team there without protective equipment. In addition, no animals in the jungle would wipe out the entire camp before they could get a distress signal out.

The next thought made more sense. Competitors.

"What are the odds a rival company sent people to steal your work?" he said.

"Hard to say. We've kept this lab very close to the chest. We've got government contracts, so interest is very high on this one. But there's always the chance. Considering the circumstances, I wouldn't rule it out."

"What about pirates or warlords in that area?"

"Negative. They would have seen signs. As I said, it's an escort mission. Get our specialist to the lab and back in one piece—and with the data, of course. All in all, it should be a cakewalk."

"A cakewalk? You don't even know what occurred there," Ziler said.

"Fair enough. I'll raise the price to two-point-five. Travel expenses are on me. But I need this done immediately."

That was Jed's way of asking if he accepted the job.

Ziler stood up, groaning slightly. He was never one to say no to work unless he suspected the job to be suicide.

"Send a plane to the Ajar Air Field. My team will be there in one hour. You know where that's at?"

"I do. Thank you, Mr. Ziler. Your contact's name is Dr. Elizabeth Moore. She'll be waiting for you in our facility in Cameroon."

"She better be as good as you say," Ziler said before hanging up the phone. As he walked into the house, he sent a mass text message to his seven mercenaries. *Grab your gear. Meet at Ajar Air Field at eleven hundred.*

Next, he went into his basement and unlocked his combat gear. His fatigues, vest, and weapons had been freshly cleaned just twelve hours ago.

"Don't know why I ever bother taking this shit off."

CHAPTER 4

When Jed Pervis said the rescue team would arrive in Cameroon by morning, he wasn't exaggerating. Dr. Liz Moore watched the Sikorsky helicopter approach from the north. Some of the research staff and the local aids gathered in the field, fascinated by the large hunk of metal that sped in their direction.

The flight was a direct fourteen-hour trip from somewhere in Florida. From what she heard, the team was gathered immediately after yesterday's phone conference, took a small, private flight to Florida, where they took a company jet to Lagos, Nigeria. From there, they boarded the Sikorsky which promptly brought them to this small, isolated village.

It would be a short layover. Time was of the essence. In the past twenty-four hours, there had been no response from the research team. All attempts to radio the base went unanswered.

A hose, attached to the diesel tank meant for the generators, was prepped and ready to refuel the aircraft.

After a few short minutes, the bird was hovering over the field. Its rotors kicked up dust as it carefully descended. As soon as it touched down, the fuselage door opened.

Out came Samuel Ziler.

Liz had spent much of the night reviewing the files on each member of the team. Jed Pervis made sure to have as many details on anyone who worked for him, whether through direct employment or off the books. He always managed to find some kind of dirt to use in case someone dared to turn against him. Fortunately, that didn't seem to be the case for Ziler. After all, he focused primarily on rescue missions, making it clear there was a line he didn't cross. No assassinations, abductions, torture, drug smuggling and so forth. A mercenary with a conscience.

Captain Samuel Ziler's appearance perfectly resembled the picture in his files. He had a somewhat lean, muscular build. Not too bulky, but unmistakably cut, even under his body armor and gear. He wore aviator sunglasses, held an M27 Infantry Automatic Rifle in his left hand, and a Beretta 9mm in his holster. A marine of twenty years, he had served in Libya, Iraq, Afghanistan, among other, lesser-known areas. Like many active-duty warriors, he worked alongside contractors who were making a great deal more for doing essentially the same work. Not one to work the typical nine-to-five job, he finished out his second term and started up his own business.

His seven mercenaries followed him onto the field.

The first was Graves. With a buzzcut and a mild burn near his left eye, he perfectly resembled the photo in his file—including the same snarky grin. He lived for the job, and unlike his boss, he had no problem with the dirty side of the business. Whoever typed out his file felt the need to include at the end: *real pain in the ass.*

A total contrast was Wallington. An average-sized man, he was the medic of the group. His training came from serving in the U.S. Air Force as a paramedic for four years. Prior to that, he was an EMT in his local community. He was the compassionate type, eager to save lives instead of taking them. In Liz's estimation, that trait was probably what led him to Samuel Ziler's team.

Next was Ankrum, a heavy gunner. The former marine was a walking stereotype. He was a mountain of a man, carrying an M60 machine gun in one hand and an ammo box with six hundred rounds in the other. Strapped over his shoulder was his secondary weapon, an HK G36. He was the first of the bunch to utter a word.

"Howdy."

The next to speak was Morales, the team mechanic. "Yo!" He followed Ankrum out of the aircraft, carrying an M4A1 Carbine in his arms and a repair kit on his back.

No words were spoken by the next mercenary. Referred to by his teammates as 'Shredder', Dawson Browne wore a metallic mask over his face. It was easier on the eyes than what was underneath it. According to his file, the Army Ranger had taken a machine gun bullet to the face. Even with his jaw literally hanging by a few strands, the bastard kept on fighting, literally taking out insurgents in hand-to-hand combat. For whatever reason, the guy liked his knives—something that was evident in his appearance. He had at least eight blades on him, including a push-dagger, a couple of fix-blade knives, some throwing knives, and a karambit. There was no hint of self-pity in his eyes. Even though the military did not see him fit for service, Ziler thought differently.

Descher and Medford stepped out behind them. The former had served in the British Royal Army, while the latter was in the Australian Special Forces. Both had worked in Afghanistan together and sought to make real money working as contractors. Fortunately, they had also met Samuel Ziler during their service. Years later, he tracked them down after starting his company.

In addition to their weaponry, each mercenary was equipped with knives, flashlights, basic first aid, and a radio system linked to their helmets.

As they approached, the men took the opportunity to glance at the corrals and the makeshift laboratory. Years back, it had been an old manufacturing facility, owned by some company using the villagers as cheap labor. Either it was abandoned, or Jed Pervis bought it cheap to be converted as a research lab. The surrounding area was a village full of two hundred people. Being in the middle of nowhere, most of the locals were extremely hard working and vigilant, but also malnourished and poorly educated.

By the expression on Ziler's face—even with the shades—it was clear he knew the company was using these people as test subjects for whatever medicine he was producing out here. Alas, he was not here for that. If it wasn't Jed Pervis taking advantage of these people, it would be someone else. All Ziler could do was worry about his own work.

He turned his eyes to his contact, taking a moment to study her outfit before introducing himself. The crease in his jawline conveyed his thoughts. So what if Liz was former Army? So what if she was a crack shot? In his eyes, she wasn't proven. He didn't like babysitting, especially in potential hot zones.

"Dr. Liz Moore?" he said. The tone in his voice all but confirmed those thoughts.

She extended her hand. "Mr. Ziler." He reluctantly shook it. Clearly, this merc was not in the mood for small talk. That suited Liz, for she wasn't either. She pointed her thumb toward the shack behind her. "Hope you and your boys got a nice nap during your flight, because we'll be leaving very shortly."

"We'll get plenty of sleep when we're dead," Graves said, that stupid smirk still on his face. "You the one who's tagging along?"

Liz was unsure if she wanted to answer.

"Hmm?"

Very quickly, she learned he wouldn't shut up unless she replied. Groaning, she turned to look at him.

"That's right."

"Fantastic," Graves said. "I knew there'd be some good scenery. Especially with those fatigues. Gotta say, they show off those oranges very nicely."

The statement naturally brought Liz's eyes to her own ass. Frustration accelerated the need for another fix. Originally, she thought she would be able to wait until they returned, but already, her body was craving another bump. First, she needed to get these jerks back on the chopper. The last thing she needed was a slew of comments about her habit. Especially not from a prick like Graves.

First thing's first, she knew not to give Graves the response he wanted. He was the type who enjoyed aggravating others. Ziler didn't appear to care enough to step in. So, the best course of action was to play along.

"Yeah?" She forced a smile. "Yours too."

"Aww!" Morales exclaimed. He smacked Graves on the ass, making him jump.

"Hey! What the—"

"What's the matter? Uncomfortable?" Morales said.

"Damn right I am..." Graves said, much to the amusement of his fellow team members.

"Alright, gentlemen," Ziler said. "The good doctor wants to give us a briefing. Let's get this done and go back home."

"Right this way." Liz led the men into the shack.

***

"This is Doctor William Aaron. We require immediate extraction. The compound has been breached. We have multiple fatalities. Please send help. We're under attack by..."

Seated at long, wooden tables in the shack, the team listened to the recording three times before Liz shut it off.

"Oh, that's convenient," Graves shouted from the back of the room. "Cut off right as he was about to identify the attacker."

"Didn't hear any gunfire," Morales said.

"Doesn't mean shots weren't fired," Wallington said.

Graves sniggered. "Dumbasses. Wasting time on a radio when they should've been shooting."

Wallington looked over his shoulder at the 'happy to be immature' mercenary. "These people aren't soldiers, dude. They're doctors, workers. Just people doing a job."

"You know, Wallington," Graves said, "you're a little too nice for your own good. These people work for the Lexington Corporation. Trust me, nobody's willy-nilly doing a nine-to-five, living in suburbia, raising two little boys and a—"

"Graves, will you shut the fuck up?" Ziler said. "Your voice carries."

"Yeah," Morales said. "Starting to wish you were the one wearing the Shredder mask instead of Browne."

Browne confirmed his agreement with a thumbs up, sparking laughter from some of the team members.

As they bantered, Liz projected a map onto a white screen, displaying a large area of rainforest over a hundred miles south of the village. Standing at the front of the room, she felt more as though she was giving a school lecture than a military-style briefing.

Graves was in the back, obnoxiously sniffing at the moldy leg of his desk.

"Fine lab," he muttered.

In this instance, Liz agreed with him. Still, she ignored him and went right to work.

"We're here," she said, pointing a yardstick to a small, light-green area north of the forest green glob that took up most of the map. "Down here is the Congo Jungle. We'll be taking the chopper down here." She put the yardstick down to a thin stretch of blue which cut through the green splotch of forest.

"That the Congo River?" Medford asked.

"No, that's not the Congo River, you wanker," Descher said. "Congo River's like, just short of three-thousand miles long. That thing's more like a, I don't know, a little backyard creek."

"Not quite that small, though it does connect with another river system which does link with the Congo," Liz said. "This particular system goes roughly twelve miles northeast, with a little segment that branches off and hooks all the way around. The only part of the system we care about is right here." She put the yardstick to a bend in the southwestern-most point of the river. "This is where the receiving area is located. We use it to airdrop supplies. There's enough of a clearing here for the chopper to set down."

"If there is a threat, the chopper might have to leave in a hurry," Ziler said. "We'll fast rope down and give the all-clear before you join us."

Liz inhaled, irritated with the interruption and his obvious overprotectiveness.

"From there, we'll take a supply boat up the river to the main facility," she continued. "In a nutshell, we investigate, rescue anyone we can, and I'll download the research data from the computers. Then we'll bug out, and ya'll can fuck off into obscurity if you want to."

"Oooo." Graves' stupid smile widened. "I like her even more." He pointed at a cabinet drawer that she had repeatedly backed towards over the course of the briefing. "Hey, Doc. What'ya got in there?"

"Hmm?"

He pointed at the drawer. There was a lock on it, sparking further interest. "Got something good in there, I bet."

She looked at the drawer, then back at him. "IDs, files, and such. None of which is your concern."

"Uh-huh."

"Graves…" Ziler said, his voice soft but intense. Graves chose to shut up, but still had that mischievous grin. Liz had to work all the more to quell the shakes. That damned mercenary's antics were working on exposing her Achilles heel.

It doesn't matter. Why should I care what these guys think? Let's just get this job done and over with quick.

"Have there been any reports of guerrilla activity in the area?" Ziler asked.

"Not that we're aware of," Liz said.

"Drug smugglers?"

"No. No groups at all."

"Any mental health conditions?" Wallington asked. "Someone go nuts, maybe? Cabin fever?"

"Or drug issues?" Graves added, winking.

Liz groaned. "None that we're aware of."

"Right." Graves leaned back and cupped his hands.

"How many staff?" Ziler asked.

"About a dozen," Liz said. "Mostly scientists, plus a few maintenance staff. They'll be easy to identify."

"If an armed group attacked this place, they'd be looking for something in particular," Ziler said. "What exactly are they working on down there?"

"Vaccine development," Liz said.

The slightest hint of a grin took form on Ziler's face. The promptness of her answer made it clear that the response was scripted, and that the truth was meant to be kept secret.

Ziler chose not to press the issue. This was a rescue mission, and the audio recording confirmed that there was someone in need of rescue. That was the only thing that mattered at the moment.

"Is the chopper refueled?"

"Yes," Liz said.

Ziler stood up and went for the door. "Then let's get to it."

Liz remained by the drawer, taking her sweet time to power down the electronics while the team filed out the door.

Graves was the last to leave, watching Liz while he stalled.

"Need help there? I'm good with, whatever it is you're pretending to do."

Liz popped an altoid tablet. It did little to quell the fix, but for some reason, those were her go-to when the desired substance was unavailable.

"I'm just finishing up," she said.

"Graves? Get out here!" Ziler called from outside.

The mercenary clicked his tongue at Liz, winking at the drawer before stepping outside.

She waited, frustrated and humiliated. The habit had gotten so bad, that even a low-life like Graves could identify it after only twenty minutes of meeting her.

At this point, she chose not to care. She unlocked the drawer, took a bump of her stash, and waited for the effects to kick in. At this point, she was no longer chasing a high. It was all about keeping the effects of withdrawal at bay. The drug entered the brain and converted to morphine. The 'pleasure rush' came, eliminating the shakes for the time being.

Hearing approaching footsteps, she quickly tucked a bag of heroin into her back pocket for the road.

Ziler poked his head in and yanked his aviators off. "You coming, Doc? I thought you were the one in a rush?"

"Uh… yeah! Yeah! Coming right now."

She double-checked her ammunition, then followed him out the door and into the Sikorsky. After strapping herself in, Liz downed half a water bottle.

"Thirsty?" Wallington said.

"It's Africa," she replied. "What do you think?"

Graves sniggered, tempted to reply to that question. Wallington broke eye contact. Being a medic, he knew what was really going on. Again, Liz did not care. Everyone had their vices. All that mattered in the end were results.

"Pilot, let's move it, will ya?!" she said.

"You're the boss."

The chopper lifted off the ground and went south. After a few minutes, the horizon was nothing but dense green jungle. Somewhere in that jungle was the Lexington Research Facility.

CHAPTER 5

After thirty miles of travel, there was not a speck of the landscape in sight that wasn't forest green. The trip consisted of the usual banter between the team members, who were eager to stretch their legs following the seemingly nonstop flying of the last fifteen hours.

Ziler watched out the window as though on a car trip. In his vest pocket were three cigars, the first of which would be lit the moment they touched down. It was a vice which kept him relaxed under pressure. On certain missions, he had to do without them due to stealth. This time, he did not concern himself.

Seated across from him was Dr. Liz Moore. His discerning glances were hidden behind his dark aviators. In the world of combat, he developed a sixth sense. Trustworthiness was an essential part of team efforts, and already, he did not trust this liaison. Like Graves, he saw the twitches and jerky, hurried movements and had heard the quick, stuttering voice—all of which suddenly went away after they stepped out of the shack.

There was still a hint of anxiety, displayed by the continuous tapping of her fingers against her leg while she watched the window.

"Everything alright, Doctor?" Ziler asked.

"Yes, I'm fine," she replied. "Just eager to get to the bottom of this situation."

"Perhaps you should wait on the chopper."

Liz's gaze pierced his aviators, her brow furrowing. "Pardon me, but did you not pay attention to our briefing back there?"

"Oh, he did," Graves muttered.

"Nobody asked you," Liz said. She turned her attention back to Ziler. "If you have concerns, Captain, list them."

"How long since your last combat deployment, and how many have you been on?" he said.

"Why does that matter?" she said.

"Answer the question."

"Unless I'm mistaken, the company is ordering that I go along," Liz said.

"And I can change my mind any moment I want," Ziler replied.

Liz sighed loudly. They were only a few minutes into this mission and already she was fed up with this team.

"Two deployments. Three combat missions," she said. "Palm Grove, Dragon Strike, and Shewan."

"The Battle of Palm Grove was in 2010," Ziler said.

"Yeah?"

"It's been twelve years."

"And?"

Ziler shrugged, not budging to her attitude. "I just want to make sure you won't crack under pressure if things go sideways down there. There's a reason I prefer to work only with my team. They're reliable. I trust them. Even Graves."

"Hey-hey!" Graves gave a thumbs up, expecting praise from his fellow mercenaries. Getting nothing, he leaned back in his seat and blew raspberries.

"What makes you think I'm not re—" Liz cut herself off, not wanting Ziler to voice the answer to that question. "I don't talk about my deployments. There's a reason for that. There's plenty of shit I wish I could unsee. Things I'm not even allowed to disclose without having Uncle Sam up my ass."

"Literally, or…"

Liz glared at Graves, who shrugged nonchalantly.

"I mean, some women like it through the back door—"

"I can demonstrate my marksmanship right now, if you'd like," Liz snapped, tilting her head in Graves' direction.

Ziler smirked. "Maybe another time."

Morales raised his hand. "When she's done, can I join in?"

"Just aim for the jaw. That's all we really need," Ankrum said. He elbowed Browne, who was seated next to him. "This guy knows what we're talking about."

Browne raised a middle finger.

"Great, great. Good to have friends," Graves said.

"Yes. Yes, it is," Medford said.

"Maybe one day you'll know what it's like," Descher added.

Graves snorted, seeing the Aussie and Brit seated together. "Are we talking about platonic friendships or are we circling back to anal sex?"

Wallington shook his head, embarrassed for the team.

"Forgive this guy," he said to Liz. "He's a crack shot. Just not with jokes."

"Or with any other aspect of his personality," Morales said.

"Oh, you're all so nice," Graves said. "I'll remember that next time one of you gets hit by grenade shrapnel. Ankrum, I seem to recall you needing roughly sixty stitches over in Cambodia."

"I did that," Wallington said.

"Yeah, but who dragged his big heavy ass over to you?" Graves said.

"I wish it was Ziler," Ankrum said. "At least he wouldn't have bumped me against four tree trunks along the way."

"Oh, you big, ungrateful baby," Graves said. He looked out the window at the world of dense rainforest.

It was a relatively clear day, though he could see rainclouds in the distant horizon. "Who'd want to work all the way out here? Middle of nowhere, surrounded by things that want to eat your eyes, God knows how many diseases."

"That's the whole point," Liz said. "Our team of specialists are developing live-saving cures, not only for the people of this continent, but all across the world. The Congo Rainforest, as well as the Amazon, contain so many undiscovered species of flora. For all we know, it may hold the cure for cancer."

"You're the head of this operation, correct?" Wallington asked.

"Yes," she said.

"Why aren't you there with the team?" he said.

"Because, we have more than one facility in the region, like the one in the village," Liz said. "Developing new vaccines requires a lot of time, a lot of work…"

"A lot of testing," Wallington added.

Liz clenched her jaw, ready to debate the ethics of the implication.

Before she could, Ziler stepped in. "What exactly are your specialties, Dr. Moore?"

"Virology and microbiology," Liz said.

"Basically, the study of viruses," Ziler said.

Liz nodded. "Mmhmm. How they work, how they spread, how fast they spread, what parts of the body they target, how to develop antivirals that can combat them…"

Graves coughed. "How to manufacture them." He 'un-strangled' his voice and looked innocently at the disgruntled Liz Moore. "Pardon me. *Clearly,* I was referring to the antivirals."

Liz chose not to engage, instead turning her eyes out her window. "About another hundred miles to go. We should be at the landing zone in roughly thirty minutes."

The finger tapping on her leg resumed.

CHAPTER 6

It was precisely thirty minutes later when they arrived at the destination. From high above, the dock area was a near-perfect circle in the middle of the rainforest. Down below were three docks, extending thirty feet into the river. The Mort de Douze Milles had a steady flow. The water had a slight green shade to it and was moving northeast toward its juncture with the Congo River.

Much of the area was dark due to overshade from the canopy. The thick vegetation, consisting of ebony, limba, wenge, and mahogany trees, competed for the sunlight. The underbrush below stretched high, struggling to absorb whatever bits of sunlight that broke through the emergent and canopy layers of rainforest.

The only sights Samuel Ziler cared about was human activity. From two hundred feet high, there did not appear to be anyone in sight. Only one supply boat—a thirty-foot barge—was moored at the docks. There was a small receiving building with a radio antenna stationed a few meters inland. From what Ziler could see through his binoculars, there was no movement.

"Time to work," he said.

He and Browne were the first to fast-rope down. As soon as their feet hit the ground, the two men branched out in search of hostiles. Descher and Medford were next, then Graves and Wallington. Morales and Browne followed.

The team formed a perimeter and secured the area. Ziler checked the north side of the clearing, then turned his attention to the barge. The paint on its hull was dried and chipping away, its white color now looking brown and covered in algae. Two fuel drums stood side-by-side on the forward deck. The flying bridge was on the stern of the vessel, its main deck heavily marked from heavy crates and wooden pallets.

Most importantly, nobody was on it.

Ziler looked at his team members. Graves, Ankrum, and Browne all gave him a thumbs up. No hostile activity. The area was secured.

The only point of question was the shack. Wallington stood by it, his H&K pointed at the closed door. At that moment, Ziler realized what had the medic concerned. The building had two window panels, both of which were shattered.

"Sir?"

Ziler was already on approach. He stopped as he arrived within ten feet of the building. A vile smell hit his nose. Over the years, Ziler and his mercenaries had smelled rotting flesh before, from animals and humans, but never this pungent.

"Form up on the door," he said to his men.

Once everyone was in position, Ziler kicked the door in. He breached the building, weapon pointed.

What he found looked almost alien. Two bodies, wearing white work shirts, lay on the floor. At first glance, Ziler suspected these men had been dead for weeks. Yet, it had only been a day since the distress signal.

Their color was completely gone, their flesh dry, yet oily at the same time. Flies and other insects helped themselves to the bodies, picking at the shrunken eyeballs, tongues, and the rest.

Graves peeked inside. "Blech!"

"Dude, come on," Wallington said.

Ziler glanced at the shattered glass, then at the back wall. There were no bullet hits. It was not gunfire that broke those windows, but a single impact which delivered massive brute force.

The men, even in death and decay, were arched backward. Their putrid stomachs were hyperextended, forming little mountains. They did not appear to be potbellies, but rather an accumulation of insides. Both areas of swelling had a single puncture wound at the top.

Ziler stepped out. "Wallington? Take an assessment." He looked to the chopper. "Dr. Moore, the area is secured. Make your descent."

Liz stood at the open fuselage door, braced herself for the long drop, then made her way down. Her descent was a little clumsy, but she managed to complete it without splattering herself all over the docks.

"What's the matter?" she said, seeing some of the men gathered by the shack.

"Two bodies. Both have company nametags," Ankrum said.

"Shot?"

He tightened his jaw and tilted his head. "N-not exactly."

Liz lifted her radio from her vest and looked to the chopper. "Return to the village and await our call."

The chopper turned north and disappeared behind the blockade of trees.

With one hand resting on her sidearm, Liz approached Ziler. "So, there was an attack?"

"Of sorts."

Liz winced. "Of sorts? The hell are you talking about?"

"They were hiding in there. Something broke in and killed them," Ziler said. "No signs of gunfire. It almost looks as though they've had their fluids drained."

Wallington stepped out of the shack. "That's exactly what happened."

"Wait, you're saying they've had their blood suctioned out?" Liz said.

"You're the one who works here, lady," Graves said.

"Developing new vaccines to cure illnesses," Liz said. "Not... this."

Ziler stepped closer to the barge. It was not aligned with the docks, but instead had been run aground in a hurry.

"Whatever happened, those poor gentlemen took a boat here in a rush," he said. "They didn't even bother anchoring or mooring it. That transmission came from the main facility, not here? Correct, Doctor?"

"Correct," Liz said.

"Whatever happened over there, these men were making a run for it," Ziler continued. "From what I can make out, something followed them here and..." He tilted his head at the broken windows, "...did that."

"It wasn't warlords, that's for damn sure," Wallington said. He waved his hand over his nose in a vain attempt to rid himself of the smell. "Oddly enough, those bodies are a day old at most. Don't think the rebel groups in the areas are in the business of syphoning blood."

"Even more interesting is the status of the boat," Ziler said. He waded through the water, getting knee-deep by the time he reached the barge. He climbed aboard and lifted an axe off the deck. There was a green, slimy substance crusting at the edge of the blade. "Not exactly normal."

He checked the cockpit. The engine had been left on, having stalled at some point in the several hours since it ran aground. He started it back up. The engine sputtered several times before finally coming to life. The fuel gauge was at one-quarter tank.

Ziler looked to his men. "Ankrum, Browne, help me dig this bad boy out. Once it's free, we'll board the boat and take it to the facility. The rest of you, maintain a perimeter. Maintain three-sixty-degrees of awareness."

While his boss worked on dislodging the boat, Wallington patrolled the northern edge of the clearing. The ground was heavily marked by the treads of bulldozers and other construction vehicles that leveled the ground and cleared out the vegetation.

He still could not get that smell out of his nose. Having served as a medic both in the military and as a civilian, he was not squeamish in the slightest. He had treated people who had been shot, burned, stabbed, crushed, blown apart, suffered chemical burns, and so much more—but never a fresh corpse drained of all fluid.

Those deaths were not natural. It only required basic logic to connect whatever happened to those men with whatever Lexington's scientists were working on up the river.

Wallington sniffed again. *Wait a sec...*

His mind wasn't playing games with him. That smell was coming from somewhere in the jungle. Wherever it was coming from, it matched the odor on those bodies exactly. Immediately, he suspected more bodies were laying beyond the clearing.

There were no footprints on the ground that he could see. The only way to know for sure was to check himself.

He pierced the tree line, surrounding himself with vegetation. So far, there was nothing unusual. It was just another day in the Congo rainforest, complete with a natural soundtrack. Turaco birds and malachite kingfishers chirped and sang, their echoes matched by the calls from sun-tailed monkeys. Aside from the humidity, he found it to be a gorgeous environment. The forest floor was much more colorful than the canopy area, with purple and yellow flowers blossoming where the light touched.

Had it not been for the presence of the two oddly drained corpses, he would have found this scenery enjoyable. In reality, this beautiful landscape was the setting for something dreadful. Possibly sinister.

New sounds caught his attention.

Between the chirps and cries were sounds of movement, mostly within the trees. Leaves quivered, branches waved, and birds fluttered their wings as they took to the air.

Something was up there.

Then there was another sound, one that seemed completely out of place. It came from within the canopy. Though not exactly alike, it reminded him of the droning sound from chopper rotors. Unlike that, however, this drone had more of a buzzing effect…

… much like the mosquito flying into his ear.

Wallington slapped the side of his head, then looked at the splattered remains on his palm.

"Gotcha, you little bastard."

The droning continued, still high in the trees. Wallington, his adrenaline starting to kick in, raised his H&K.

What the hell is that?

"Psst!"

Wallington turned around, ready to blow holes in the stupid moron known as Graves. The grin on his face wavered only slightly, his eyebrows raised high when he saw the gun muzzle briefly pointed in his direction.

He pointed a finger upward at a tree branch thirty degrees off Wallington's right shoulder. The medic slowly looked. Right away, he saw the golden fur and brown eyes of a rainforest leopard. It was eyeing the human, ready to pounce until the second one arrived.

Graves stepped beside Wallington with a rock in hand. "Get out of here, *Sabor*." He chucked the rock, hitting the cat square in the face. It snarled and retreated to the next branch.

Wallington exhaled slowly, feeling foolish for not noticing the thing beforehand. Not even the realization of nearly getting jumped by a predator took his mind off the oddity that had caught his attention moments earlier.

He looked to the sky and listened. That strange sound in the trees was gone.

"You're welcome," Graves said.

"Did you hear anything?" Wallington said.

"Yeah. The cat licking its gums," Graves said. "The hell are you doing out here, anyway? *Trying* to get yourself killed?"

"I thought I heard something," Wallington said. He listened again. Whatever it was, it was gone now. Perhaps it was his imagination playing tricks on him. The only thing he was certain of was the smell. "I think there's another body out here."

"Yeah, it would've been yours had it not been for me," Graves said.

Wallington continued scanning the forest. "No, but there's something…"

"The jungle's full of dead things, Wallington," Graves said. The sound of a motor drew their attention to the river. "We'd better head back." He tapped Wallington on the shoulder and returned to the clearing.

Wallington took another whiff. While it was clear another body was out here, locating it would be a waste of time. The better course of action would be to report it to Ziler and investigate once they returned to rendezvous with the copter.

After giving one last glance at the trees, he rejoined his teammates at the river. The boat was refueled and aligned with the dock with Ziler at the helm. His cigar was planted between his teeth, its tip bright orange as he drew on it.

"Mount up, ladies. Let's go, let's go, let's go. This is already taking longer than I care for. Wallington, why are you so slow?"

"Sorry, Captain."

Ziler removed the cigar from his mouth. "Something the matter?"

"It can wait." Wallington stepped aboard the barge. "I'll explain on the way."

With everyone on deck, Ziler turned the boat around and throttled northeast up the river.

"Keep your heads on a swivel, gentlemen," the Captain said. "Watch the shore. Report if you see anything."

"Nah, I thought I'd keep it to myself," Graves said.

Meanwhile, Ankrum took position on the bow deck. With his M60 propped up on its bipods, the barge now had the appearance of a gunboat. Fed by an ammo chain, the weapon was ready to unload two-hundred rounds at anything that dared to challenge the team.

Liz stood near the portside, her altoid container in her hand. Two of them were crushed in her teeth.

Ziler shook his head. He would never look at the mints the same way ever again.

***

The big cat found a sturdy branch which pointed out toward the river. From there, it watched the humans, all gathered on the floating object. Its brow was sore from where the rock had struck it. Pain triggered its aggression. Had it not been for the presence of multiple humans in the area, it would have pounced on the offender and gleefully sank its fangs into his jugular.

It had tasted human once before. Two years back, it had located a group of explorers. One of them wandered off from the group. It seemed to be a perfect opportunity. It descended from the trees and drove the clumsy human to the ground. Teeth sank into the back of its prey's neck in search of the jugular vein. The victim had let out a loud cry, attracting the others in his party. One of them carried a large stick-shaped object.

The leopard remembered the loud *bang* that came from the weapon. The projectile had missed it, but the lesson was learned. Hunting humans was probably not worth the effort.

Still, it remembered the taste. When hungry, humans looked as enticing as the warthogs, monkeys, and other species it hunted.

It watched until the boat moved out of sight.

A heavy buzzing sound alerted the leopard. It stood up on the branch, the hair on its back rising on end. The sound was coming from directly above it.

It had seen this fiend before. Like now, the flying insectoid had descended from the heavens and swooped down onto an unsuspecting warthog. The cat had been tracking the beast with intent to pounce and rip into it, only for this seemingly alien species to beat it to the punch.

Normally, it would fight for possession of the meal. However, it only took a few moments of watching the blur of flailing legs and wings to make the cat reconsider. It chose to protect its own life and hunt elsewhere.

It was a choice that only bought it a day's worth of life.

The cat looked up.

The droning intensified. The thing was directly above it, its shape blocking out the rays of sun. Six legs, long and narrow, outstretched from its thorax.

Leaping from branch to branch, the leopard retreated. In under a few moments, it crossed over a dozen meters of distance. Yet, the assailant continued closing in.

The buzzing was louder than ever. Air pushed by the fluttering wings brushed against its back. Panicked, the cat attempted to leap to another tree. The landing was clumsy and unsuccessful. It hit the trunk, its claws penetrating the bark. A combination of instinct and fear caused the animal to cling to the side of the tree, unintentionally making it a prime target.

Thin legs closed in over its shoulders and ribs. Before the cat could retaliate, a piercing pain struck the back of its neck. Like the human it had nearly slain two years ago, it let out a deafening cry.

It felt its insides compressing, the flesh sinking between its bones. Its vision went dark as its eyes shriveled into their sockets. The attacker's hideous abdomen pressed against the small of the leopard's back, swelling as it filled with blood.

Finished, it withdrew its proboscis and took to the skies.

The cat, now bone thin, fell from the tree. It hit the ground, settling next to the bloodless corpses of two gorillas, their rank bodies permeating the air.

CHAPTER 7

Thump!

Graves peeked over the bow, having felt the reverberation of some kind of impact against the hull.

"There it is again."

"There *what* is again?" Morales asked.

Graves shot a glare at the mechanic. It was the second time he felt a bump against the bottom of the boat, and also the second time Morales did not notice.

"The hell you mean 'what'?" Graves said. "Didn't you feel that?"

"I felt it this time," Ankrum said.

"Relax, gentlemen," Liz said. "We probably bumped against a piece of wood or something."

"Felt more like something came up to the boat," Graves said. He walked along the edge of the boat, monitoring the water on the starboard side.

Ziler watched from the flying bridge. They had traveled two miles upriver with no signs of hostile life. He had faintly felt the thump as well. His first instinct was to agree with Liz. It seemed unlikely there was anything in the water that would cause them harm. On the other hand, he agreed with Graves—it felt like something had specifically come up and bumped against the boat.

All he knew for sure was that something unnatural had occurred in this jungle. A few minutes after leaving the dock area, Wallington explained his suspicion of other bodies in the jungle near the shack. Though it was unconfirmed, Ziler trusted the medic's judgement.

"Nothing over here," Wallington said. He was peering over the portside, looking left at the water near the stern area. The sound of a splash made him do a double-take. "Wait... hold on a sec..."

Medford and Descher joined him.

"Whoa!" Medford pointed. "You see that?"

"Looked like a fin," Descher said.

By the time everyone else looked, all they saw was a tiny swell several meters behind the boat.

"Could've been a big bass for all we know," Morales said.

Liz chuckled. "First of all, there's no bass in Africa. All it takes are five brain cells to know that."

Graves pointed obnoxiously at Morales. "Ha-ha. Now we know who uses only four brain cells."

Liz looked at him. "And, in my estimation, it only takes *one* brain cell to know there's nothing large enough in this river that can threaten this boat. Gosh, you act as though there's a great white shark circling the boat."

Graves sneered, thinking which of the numerous vulgar responses forming in his mind would get him in least trouble with Ziler.

Thump!

This time, even Liz felt it.

Her hand went to her holster, her eyes to the water. "Wait a sec..."

Ziler perked up. "Visual contact. One o'clock off the starboard side bow, six meters."

All eyes turned. This time, everyone saw the thin, rounded dorsal fin and the pointed upper lobe of what clearly was a fish's tail—a *huge* fish's tail. It turned toward the boat and fluttered its caudal fin.

Its body, light brown in color and over twenty feet long, was cigar-shaped. It increased speed as it approached, intent on ramming the vessel.

41

"Heads up!" Ankrum said, bracing for impact.

THUMP!

This time, there was no mistaking the creature's intent. The previous bumps may have been the fish curiously investigating the boat. Now, it was intent on sinking it.

Browne snapped his fingers, gaining the attention of his teammates. He pointed to the starboard quarter, where the fish was circling around.

Morales hurried to the bow and looked over the side to check for any damage. "Don't see a breach... oh SHIT!"

The fish swam up the length of the boat, raising its pointy head as it neared the tasty human. Its jaws parted, showing off their razor-sharp teeth.

Ankrum grabbed him by the collar and yanked him back. Morales squealed as he fell backward.

The jaws snapped shut where his head had been a split-second earlier. Seizing nothing but humid air, the fish splashed down. Its caudal fin slapped the side of the boat as it made a sharp turn.

Ziler took a firing position from the flying bridge. He centered the dorsal fin in the crosshairs of his M27 and squeezed the trigger.

Flesh and blood splattered from the creature's back. Spurred by pain, the fish dipped under the water.

Ziler, with his weapon still holstered, followed the trail of blood. The fish ducked under the boat, emerging on the port side. Graves was in place, ready and waiting. Several bullets spat from the muzzle of his HK416, striking the creature in the side.

It raised its head and shook side to side, snapping its jaw at the air. The fish was agitated and confused all at once. Not understanding the functionality of firearms, it did not understand how the humans were inflicting pain on it from a distance.

All it knew was survival. In some instances, the only way to survive was to kill. Being a wounded animal, it was twice as deadly as before.

The fish turned around and charged at the boat. Its beady eyes caught sight of the human on board.

Graves shouted "Oh, shit!" and sprinted across the deck.

The fish breached, crushing that portion of the guardrail as it crashed on deck.

The boat shook, then teetered to port, shaking as the fish proceeded to thrash about.

All eight team members took aim and unloaded into the thing.

Bang! Bang! Bang! Bang! Bang! Bang! Bang!

The fish juddered from the barrage of impacts, spitting globs of blood and minced meat onto the deck.

Ziler centered his crosshairs on the creature's right eye.

Bang!

SPLAT!

The eye—and the brain behind it—splattered. The fish settled on its left side, its body carved by the bombardment. Shell casings rolled across the deck, some still trailing smoke.

Fresh magazines were loaded into the weapons. For a few moments, everyone waited in stunned silence, all at once absorbing the phantastic sight slumped over the deck.

Graves looked to Liz. "So, Doc... you were saying something about no big fish in the water?"

"The hell is that thing?" Medford said.

"A fish!" Graves said. "A *big* fish!"

"Yeah, I know," Medford said.

"What he meant was, 'How'd this fish get so big, and where the hell did it come from?'" Descher said.

"Ask the Doc," Graves said.

Liz backed away. "Me?"

"Oh, right," Graves said. "Science lab, distress signal, giant fish… anyone sensing a connection."

"You think the fish chased those men to the shack and sucked their blood?" Morales said with a smirk.

"Well, no, but…"

"Enough." Ziler slowed the boat to a stop, then stepped down on the main deck. He examined the creature's jaws and the stake-like teeth inside. He planted his boot on the tip of its snout and pushed.

Wallington and Ankrum assisted, successfully ridding the barge of this monstrosity.

The boat leveled out, its deck cracked where the thing had crashed down. They watched the twenty-foot corpse drift along the surface before submerging.

"It's an African pike," Ziler said.

Graves chuckled. "You a fish expert now, boss?"

"He's been here before," Wallington said. "Plus he's smart enough to learn all aspects of the environment during the flight. Including wildlife."

"Alright, kiss-ass," Graves said. "Answer me this, then. In your reading, Captain, did you happen to learn anything about twenty-foot pike?"

Ziler shook his head. "Nope. Not in any of my literature." He looked to Liz. "Doctor, you have any explanations you'd like to share?"

Liz scoffed and headed to the deckhouse. "Just get us to the lab, will ya?" She went inside and hid in the galley.

"So… she's really gonna act like this was a perfectly normal occurrence, isn't she?" Medford said.

"Looks that way," Ziler replied. "How does the damage look, Medford?"

With caution, having nearly had his head bitten off a few minutes ago, Medford peeked over the port side to inspect the hull.

"No breach that I can see. I'll go below to make sure," he said.

"What's next?" Ankrum said.

"We keep going," Ziler said. "What? You expect a big fish to void our mission?"

"Hell no, sir," Ankrum said. "I'm just concerned about encountering another big pike."

"If we do, then we shoot it too." Ziler returned to the flying bridge. He pushed the throttle forward, accelerating the boat. "Hopefully, that pike is the strangest thing we encounter on this trip."

'Hopefully' was the key word.

CHAPTER 8

They could see the pier and radio tower up ahead.

Even from three-hundred yards downriver, Ziler's team of mercenaries knew they were nearing a mass grave. The odor radiating off the bodies at the docks was present here, wafting the length of the river as though to greet them. It was just as rank as it was near the shack, steadily getting worse as they neared the pier.

Ankrum took position on his machine gun, taking aim at the landing zone. So far, there was no movement.

The rest of the team stood ready to storm the property. They kept low, preparing for any surprises.

If this trip had taught them anything, it was that it was full of surprises.

As he steered the boat toward the pier, Ziler kept a watchful eye on the water. The last thing he or his team needed was a surprise attack from another giant fish.

"Ankrum, provide cover. Browne, Medford, and Descher, take the west side. The rest of you, on me. We'll secure the perimeter first, then inspect the facility. Dr. Moore, you stay by me at all times."

She had emerged from the galley, noticeably relaxed. Standing at the steps which led to the flying bridge, she unholstered her pistol and waited behind Browne, Medford, and Descher. Every man had their primary weapon aimed at the property, ready to fire on any threat, man or animal.

They arrived at the pier.

The Lexington Research Facility was comprised of three main buildings: the two-story research lab, the greenhouse, and maintenance shed. The latter two were on the west side of the clearing, with a large generator unit standing between them and the main building.

To the left of the pier was the radio tower, stretching at over sixty feet into the gap in the canopy. Grouped at its legs were eight diesel drums, containing the fuel supply for the outpost.

The research building was a fairly large structure, with a height of over twenty feet and covering at least five thousand square feet. The effort to construct this place in the middle of the rainforest had to have been a strenuous effort, with resources flown in and floated down the Congo River. And, judging by the obvious damage sustained from some kind of attack, a wasted effort.

Ziler could see shattered windows on both levels. There was some markings on the sidings, but overall, the damage was limited to the window panels. There were no bullet holes or other signs of an armed attack. The roof tiles were in disarray, with several peeled off and scattered all over the ground.

From what Ziler observed, whoever—or *whatever*— attacked this place seemed to fixate on the second floor.

The only sign of life were the flies buzzing over the three bodies in the yard. One of them was belly-down near the pier, hands outstretched in the direction of the boat. His eyes shrunken into his skull and his jaw outstretched as though screaming, the image of his last moments was hauntingly illustrated. Between his shoulders was a single puncture wound.

"Let's go. Move it out," Ziler said.

The mercenaries stormed the property. Ankrum kept his machine gun centered on the building while Browne, Descher, and Medford flanked left.

Ziler led the second group ashore, sweeping to the right to secure the east and north side of the property. All they found were two more corpses, one slumped in the cab of a forklift, the other on his back, his bony hands clinging to a bolt-action rifle.

Ziler knelt by the second body and pried the weapon from his hands. He opened the bolt, the extractor kicking out an empty case into the grass. He opened the floor plate where the ammo was loaded into the weapon. There was nothing inside.

He placed the weapon down and glanced at Wallington. "Every cartridge has been fired."

"East side's secure," Medford said into his earpiece. *"Got two bodies in the greenhouse, sucked dry just like the others."*

"Copy that. Two bodies on west side in similar condition," Ziler said.

"And Captain, uh... Not sure if this is worth mentioning, but we've got what looks like a paddock over here."

"Like for livestock?"

"Yeah. Got a couple of dead things in it. Thought they were goats at first, but they look more like..."

"Rats," Descher said for him. *"BIG rats."*

"Sucked dry just like the personnel," Medford said.

Ziler looked to Liz, who offered no explanation. Whatever it was the team was really working on out here, she didn't want anyone to know. She tilted her head at the building with an impatient manner, obviously eager to access the computers. She could not give less of a shit regarding the loss of life. In her eyes—and the eyes of the company—humans were apparently replaceable. The product, on the other hand...

"Medford, continue sweeping the outside perimeter. We're gonna check the main lab and get Dr. Moore's data. Ankrum, stay on that machine gun. Don't let the quiet fool you, gentlemen." Ziler stood up and led his team around the front of the building.

They formed up on the door, peeking through the broken window. Inside was another body, lying face-down on the carpet. His cheek was flayed open, the carpet crusted with his blood, as if he had been slashed with a machete before having his fluids drained.

Up ahead was the main hall, leading to a variety of rooms. At the far end of that hall were two double doors. Three separate doors lined the left side, spaced roughly twelve feet apart.

Finally, Liz spoke up. "Labs One, Two, and Three, are on the left side," Liz said. "Middle door on the right leads to a separate hall, which connects to the dining and kitchen areas. Behind those double doors is storage."

"And upstairs?" Ziler said.

"Crew quarters on the west side of the hall, conference room, radio room, and offices on east side," Liz said.

Ziler looked to Morales and Graves, then tilted his head at the stairwell entrance at the corner of the room. The two mercenaries ascended to the upper level, leaving Ziler, Wallington, and Liz to sweep the first floor.

***

With muzzles tilted upward at forty-five-degree angles, the two mercs scaled the steps. The door at the top of the stairs was ajar, the hallway behind it silent. Graves took point, gently pushing the door open. Confirming nothing was on the other side, he pressed inward.

He and Morales emerged in a long hallway which stretched the length of the building. As the doctor had informed him, the crew quarters were on the left side, the offices and conference area on the right.

Graves peeked into the nearest bedroom, staying in the doorway. It was empty, the bed well made, the closet open and organized. Whoever occupied this room was probably elsewhere when the attack occurred. For all of Lexington's faults, they at least made the effort to give their employees a somewhat luxurious stay. Each staff member had their own private quarters, complete with a small desk area.

Graves and Morales went room to room in a futile attempt to search for survivors. On the opposite side was an open door with a harsh odor pouring into the hallway.

They entered the room, finding two bodies on the floor next to some radio equipment. One was female, the other male—both pasty white and void of fluid. The window had been shattered, the equipment knocked off the desk onto the floor, the carpet mangled where the staff members met their end. The man, judging by the white coat he wore, was one of the scientists working here.

Graves knelt by one of the bodies and checked the nametag on the jacket. "Dr. William Aaron." He looked at Morales. "Name sound familiar?"

Morales nodded. "The guy who made the distress call."

"Well, now we have an idea as to why that call stopped short." Graves stood up and looked at the busted window. The glass was all over the floor, meaning whatever force that shattered it came from the outside.

He stuck his head outside, looking at the siding and the grass.

"Doesn't look like anything climbed up here. It's almost as though something…" he chuckled "…*flew* through this window."

Morales could not take his eyes off Dr. Aaron's dry corpse. Insects had come in and were picking at his eyes and tongue.

"What's big enough to fly through a window and suck this guy's blood?" he muttered.

50

Graves, still looking out the window, turned his gaze to the river. The memory of that giant pike flashed in his mind. He was no scientist, but he knew how to put two and two together.

"Let's hope the doctor lady downloads her bullshit off the computer quickly so we don't have to find out. Come on." Graves exited the radio room to continue their sweep of the floor. "Faster we do this, the sooner we can leave."

***

Lab Room One was the cleanroom section of the chemistry lab, designed to control contamination and aid in the removal of airborne particles. The room appeared almost futuristic in its design, with all kinds of high-tech equipment appearing perfectly clean and functional. The technology included a Panasonic cell processing workstation, Baker Class II biosafety cabinets, steri-cult incubators, Milteny CliniMACS cell separator, EVOS XL Core microscopes, CryoMed controlled rate freezers, a pharmacy refrigerator, and other chem lab equipment that Ziler was unable to name.

Ultimately, it did not matter that he did not know what this stuff was, or what exactly they were developing. One thing he often reminded himself of was the fact it was better he did not know. He slept better at night that way.

Liz entered the lab. The cleanliness of the room was contaminated with the body of a scientist. Slumped against the west wall with a single stab wound in his throat, his skeletal face seemed to stare across the room. The floor was littered with shards of broken glass and microscope fragments.

What Ziler noticed most, other than the presence of the body itself, was the denting of the ceiling tiles.

Whatever attacked these people must have been nine feet tall. That, or it was capable of flight.

Considering the condition of the roof, Ziler suspected the latter.

Liz appeared less concerned about the body than she was checking the pharmacy refrigerators. She opened each one in a hurry, muttering anxiously to herself.

"Oh, come on. Don't tell me you guys lost them…"

"Problem, Doctor?" Ziler said.

"Nothing that concerns you," she replied.

Wallington stared at the spilled contents on the floor. "We're not being exposed to airborne toxins, are we? I mean, this is a cleanroom…"

Liz took a minute to inspect a label on one of the broken vials. "No. This stuff is harmless." She went right back to checking the fridge. Opening the third one, she breathed a sigh of relief. "Oh, thank God." She snatched three vials, both made of thick glass, and tucked them in her pouch.

"The hell is that?" Wallington asked.

"None of your concern," Liz said.

Wallington and Ziler shared a glance, then shrugged in unison. Her response practically screamed the answer. It was the main product, possibly a vaccine, that was being manufactured in this lab.

After zipping the pouch shut, Liz strutted between the two mercenaries and exited into the hallway.

"No need to check Lab Two. Computers are in Lab Three. Let me download the data, then we can rendezvous with the chopper."

"After we finish sweeping the building for survivors," Ziler said.

Liz chuckled. "Captain, I think it's obvious there are none. Let's finish this up. My company is paying you quite handsomely for this quick, easy assignment."

Ziler inhaled deeply, suppressing a sigh. It was one of those moments where conscience and the job came into conflict.

"How long should this take?" he said.

"Not long. I might have to restart the computer, which'll take about two minutes. Thirty seconds to type in my password and access the files. After that, maybe ten-to-fifteen minutes to download everything I need. These computers are top of the line, so it shouldn't take longer than that."

Midway through that last sentence, Liz was heading down the hall. She passed Lab Room Two without even giving it a glance, then waited for the others to form up on Lab Room Three before entering. Exercising a little caution, she drew her Beretta, keeping it pointed at the floor while Ziler entered the room.

Lab Room Three was probably the cleanest area in the entire facility. There were no bodies or damage of any kind. Several monitors, all linked to a central processing computer, were lined on both sides of the room. The lab had essentially been left untouched in the attack, which suited Liz.

She marched to the main computer and took a seat. It had shut down automatically in the last twenty-four hours, forcing her to restart it. The computer started to whine, its monitors giving off a white light as they came to life. Pulling a thumb drive from her vest, Liz began her usual 'tapping' regimen while she impatiently waited for the machine to wake up.

Thump!

All eyes looked to the south wall.

"Movement," Wallington whispered.

"Probably nothing," Liz said.

Thump! Thump!

Something fell over and shattered. They heard the wheeling of an office chair, and the tapping of what sounded like feet against the carpet.

Ziler and Wallington hurried into the hallway. Liz, cursing under her breath, swiveled in her chair to call after them.

"Leave it be!"

"Either it's a survivor or a hostile," Ziler said. He didn't even give Liz the benefit of eye contact as he spoke. He adjusted his mic to his lips. "Graves, what's your twenty?"

"Second floor, north end. Checked all rooms. Found only bodies."

"Report to Level One, Lab Room Two. We've got movement. Attempting to identify before breaching."

"On our way."

Ziler looked at Wallington. *Ready?*

Wallington nodded. *Whenever you are.*

Ziler, his right hand aiming his weapon, knocked on the door with his right fist. "You in the room, identify yourself." He waited. No answer came. "I repeat, you in the room, IDENTIFY YOURSELF! We are a rescue team, we're here to help. If you do not respond, you may get shot."

They heard heavy movement on the other side of the door. Something else fell over. All of a sudden, they heard what sounded like a high-pitched snarl.

Graves and Morales emerged from the stairwell entrance and quickly joined their teammates in the hall, just in time to hear the 'response'.

"Doesn't sound like he likes you," Graves muttered.

"Shh." Ziler shouldered his weapon, then kicked the door in.

To their surprise, Lab Room Two was not equipped with top-of-the-line equipment and borderline-futuristic technology. On the contrary, this one resembled a poorly run dog shelter. Everywhere they looked were cages, most of them large enough to house a Great Dane. Some of their doors were busted open, the broken locks laying on the carpet.

In the center of the room were two large operating tables, the smooth surfaces marked with scratches. Operating lights, surgical trays, sedatives, and other items were scattered across the room.

On the other end of one of the tables, something shifted. Ziler's heart fluttered when he saw movement on the floor. It wasn't an arm or a leg—but what he could only describe as a giant snake. It slithered out of sight, the rest of it appearing on the right side of the table.

Graves gulped. "Holy—"

Clawed legs scratched the floor, carrying a bulky, mangy mass. A large rat, nearly five feet in body length, turned its red eyes toward the mercenaries. Huge, crooked teeth protruded from its gums.

The rodent hissed, rearing on its hind legs. It had no fear of these humans, nor the weapons they carried. Its aggression matched its size. A moment after making eye contact, the creature charged.

Bursts of gunfire shook the room.

Bullet hits stopped the rodent in its tracks. Red blood spurted from craters in its flesh, splattering across the room. Its hisses turned to agonized squeals. The rodent reeled backward, unintentionally exposing its underside to the barrage of gunfire.

The rat settled on its back, its stomach carved open, legs, mouth, and tail twitching as the brain fired its last signals.

Ziler stepped further into the room, his muzzle still pointed at the freshly dead corpse.

Graves and Wallington flanked left, sweeping around the operating tables.

"Clear!" Graves said.

"Got another body over here," Wallington said.

"Captain, report contact." It was Ankrum, radioing from the boat.

"Contact neutralized," Ziler replied. "All units outside, hold your positions. Continue monitoring perimeter."

"Copy."

"Eww," Graves muttered, looking at the exposed skull and neckbone of whoever it was that was sprawled on the floor near the cages. This victim was not suctioned of blood, but in fact was a victim of the huge rodent.

Graves glanced at all of the cages, then at the dead rat. "Looks like our buddy locked himself in here, only to serve as a meal for this little vermin."

"Not sure 'little' is the word I would use," Wallington said.

Ziler glanced at the far wall. This lab had no windows. It seemed whatever killed the others was unable to infiltrate this lab.

He took a moment to observe all the equipment in the room. There were IV drips and syringes, with storage refrigerators full of God-knows-what.

As usual, it was Graves who voiced the obvious.

"So, first a giant fish, now a giant rat…" He looked to Ziler. "Please don't tell me they were operating on monkeys here. I'd really hate to run into *King Kong.*"

"Now we know what the corral outside is for," Morales said.

"Doubt they were milking cows," Graves said. "Where's the doc?"

Morales, who remained in the hallway, glanced in the direction of Lab Room Three. "I think she's in there."

Ziler smirked. The woman never bothered to stand up from her precious computer desk.

He exited the lab and marched to the computer room. Sure enough, Liz was still in her seat. Her thumb drive was plugged in and blinking red. On the screen was a percentage dial, now reading seventeen percent. Eighteen. Nineteen. She wasn't kidding when she said the computer was fast. If Ziler had to venture a guess, there were enough terabytes in that computer to fill a city library. That thumb drive certainly did not look like the kind that could be bought at Best Buy.

"Told you not to go in," Liz said, her eyes not leaving the monitor screen.

Ziler was not in the mood for attitude. He strutted into the room in a manner aggressive enough to make the doctor back her chair up. She leaned back, her hand creeping toward her pistol as he towered over her.

"You've withheld information," he said.

"I warned you not to enter Lab Room Two…"

"Dr. Moore, shut up with the technicalities. You knew there were giant rats in this facility…"

"A sentence none of us thought we'd ever say," Graves muttered in the hallway.

"I'm not going to ask what it was you were working on," Ziler continued. "I will ask, however, if your experiments involved more, let's just say… animal experimentation."

"Not that we were experimenting on." Liz relaxed. "Just the rats. We were using their blood to produce a…" she stammered for a sec, "…a vaccine to fight tuberculosis and malaria. We used a growth hormone to enlarge the rats, that way we had access to more DNA."

Ziler clenched his teeth, forcibly stopping himself from pressing the issue. He knew her answer was partially true at most. That wasn't his concern. All he wanted to know was if there were more surprises involving overgrown wildlife.

"Can you explain the other bodies? Last time I checked, rats don't suck peoples' blood," he said.

"I... I honestly don't know."

"What about them bird cage things in that room?" Ziler said. "I doubt you were using those to store rats."

"Let me guess," Graves said. "You guys were experimenting on giant birds. Solving the world's food crisis, are we?"

Ziler spun toward the door. "Graves, shut up. Why don't you and Wallington secure the storage area?"

"On it, sir," Wallington said. He smacked Graves' shoulder, directing him to the north end of the building.

Ziler shifted his attention back to Liz. The look on her face said it all. She knew a lot more than she was letting on.

"What was in those cages?" he said.

"Nothing that's present," Liz replied. She pointed her thumb at the screen, which now read thirty-six percent complete. "It's need-to-know information. In ten minutes, you'll have absolutely zero reason to know. I'm pretty sure we'll survive until then."

Ziler snorted at that statement, then turned to walk away.

"Yep, I can tell."

Liz scowled. "Beg your pardon, Captain? 'Can tell' what?"

"That it's been a decade since you left the military." Ziler stepped into the hallway and took a right.

A lot could happen in ten minutes.

***

The *thumps* from upstairs were faint, almost otherworldly. Only the keenest ear would recognize the sounds as footsteps. Even the voices seemed distant, leaving Dr. Susan Cabot uncertain if they were even real.

For the past day, she remained crouched in the far corner, armed only with a prybar. Twenty-four hours locked in the cellar did her psyche no favors. Fear and shock had sent her brain into overdrive. People she had known for years had been brutally murdered in front of her eyes. Her time hiding was spent dwelling on the horror she had witnessed and her regret in her role in creating it. Except to use the bathroom in the opposite corner of the cellar, she hardly moved from her spot.

Then the gunshots rang out.

Susan jumped to her feet. A new burst of adrenaline surged through her veins, shocking her out of the sleep-like state of shock. She could now hear distinct chatter coming from down the main hall. Someone was, in fact, here. A rescue team, perhaps? Or, knowing Lexington Corp., possibly a cleanup team sent to retrieve the samples from Lab Room One and erase any other evidence.

Several moments of hesitation followed. If Lexington was indeed erasing evidence, revealing herself would be Susan's doom. After all, she was the only one who went on record protesting the ultimate purpose of this facility. Being an immunologist, she signed on to save lives from *existing* illnesses. That was her original objective when she agreed to be stationed in the Congo Rainforest. Over time, she learned of the company's true intention.

On the other hand, not revealing herself would mean being left here. Sooner or later, the bugs would be back. As much as she feared the company, Susan's stomach churned at the thought of being stabbed with a proboscis and feeling her blood getting vacuumed from her veins.

Shaky hands gripped the prybar. Slowly, she approached the steps.

Already, she could hear movement in the storage room. Muffled voices spoke. At least two people were in there.

Up the steps she went.

One.

Two.

Three.

Four.

Five.

Six.

At the seventh step, she was at the oak door.

Susan froze.

What if my mind's playing games with me? What if I WANT to believe it's a rescue team outside, when in fact it's more of... THEM?!

She heard the voices, now in the storage room. They were speaking low, but were clearly distinguishable. Two men were in there, probably positioned where Trent Powell and Mike Helm were killed.

Not my imagination. Someone's out there!

Her mind fixated on the ultimate question: *How friendly are they?*

A shaky hand hovered over the doorknob as she debated whether to take the chance. Anxiety acted like a shield, preventing her from making contact. That fear of being shot was as great as sharing Trent and Mike's fate.

Susan knew she could not remain in this state of limbo forever. Slowly, she managed to grip the knob.

Again, she hesitated.

Taking several deep breaths, she made her decision. She would count down from five and reveal herself.

Five...

Anxiety kicked in, triggering an adrenaline rush. Her hand quivered on the knob, juddering it, ready to yank the door open.

Four, three...

***

"Two bodies, just like the other ones," Wallington said. He checked the nametags. "Mike Helm and Trent Powell."

"Shh!" Graves tilted his chin up, his hands shifting his weapon. "You hear that?"

Wallington listened. It sounded like something was being shaken.

"It sounds like it's coming from..." He focused on the direction of the noise, turning his eyes to an oak door in the corner of the room. "There."

Graves turned to look. As soon as he laid eyes on the door, it flung open with startling force.

"Shit!"

He pointed his weapon and squeezed the trigger, only to shift his barrel upward at the last moment after he saw that it was a human emerging from the dark stairway behind the door.

The woman shrieked, hearing the collective sound of the gunshot and the bullet impacting on the wall above her head. Jumping back, she missed her step. The next shriek came as she tumbled down the stairs.

Graves pointed his weapon down. "Aw, shiiiiiiiiit!"

He and Wallington raced to the stairs. The woman was on the floor, dazed after a very bumpy fall.

Ziler stormed into the storage room, ready to start blasting at a moment's notice. He looked to the two men, standing at the cellar entrance.

"What happened?"

Wallington hurried down the steps. "Got a survivor... I think."

"You think?" Ziler's voice was never higher than in this moment.

"Ah-ah!" Graves pointed at the bullet hole above the door. "Don't look at me! I did not shoot her. Just... *at* her."

Shaking his head, Ziler approached the door. Wallington was at the woman's side, checking her head.

"How is she?"

"She'll live. She's a little dazed," Wallington said. He glanced over his shoulder into the interior of the room. "Looks like she hid in here since the incident."

Ziler looked at the bodies laying on the storage room floor. His eyes went to the walls. There were some noticeable scrapes on the wallpaper, as though a large bird had tried to grip there.

Or a giant bug.

"Graves, help me out," Wallington said.

The merc joined his comrade in the cellar, put one of the woman's arms over his shoulders, then helped her up the steps. He glanced at the nametag on her white coat.

"Dr. Susan Cabot," he said.

She had a cut on the left side of her head surrounded by redness. Her eyes closed repeatedly, slowly succumbing to unconsciousness.

"Get her into the computer lab," Ziler said.

Down the hall they went, taking a right at Lab Room Three. Morales stood outside the door, standing guard. His eyes widened as he saw the brunette in her mid-thirties, head hanging low.

"Whoa!"

He backed away, giving them a clear path through the door.

Liz turned in her seat as they entered the room, then stood up suddenly. "Dr. Cabot?!" While her voice mainly conveyed astonishment, the mercenaries' keen ears picked up a trace of resentment.

Wallington and Graves placed Susan upright in a computer chair.

"Hang on, ma'am," the medic said. He went right to work applying disinfectant on her cut. Susan winced, the firing of nerves shocking her back to life.

She nearly jumped out of her seat, stopped only by Wallington's calming voice and hand on her shoulder.

"Whoaaaa. Shh! It's alright. You're safe," he said. Susan looked around, seeing the mercenaries standing in an unthreatening manner. She took a deep breath and relaxed in her seat, wincing as Wallington continued patching her up. "Sorry for that little misunderstanding. You gave us a little scare."

Susan looked across the room at Liz, whose eyes were peering back at her. The smell of rot slowly made its way into her nostrils, sparking a whole new wave of anxiety.

"Did anyone else make it?" she asked.

"I'm afraid not," Ziler said.

Susan glanced back and forth, her breathing intensifying. "Did you kill them? Are they destroyed?"

"Hmm?" Wallington cocked his head back in surprise. "The... scientists?"

"No, no..." Susan shut her eyes, her temples still throbbing from the fall. "The experiment. The..."

"Oh, the rats?" Graves said. "Only saw one, but we took care of it."

"No, not the rats," Susan said. "The mos—"

Liz plucked the thumb drive from the computer and stepped in-between Susan and Ziler.

"Alright, Captain! I got what I need. We can extract now."

Ziler adjusted his mic. "All units, prep for evac. We got what we need, plus one survivor. Assemble at the boat in two."

"Copy that, sir," Medford responded through the comm.

"Hang on a sec," Ziler said, raising his hand. He looked to Susan. "What happened?"

Liz smacked his hand down. "Not your concern."

Ziler raised his hand again, this time pointing a finger at her face.

"If there's a possibility we're going to run into whatever attacked this place, then damn right it's my concern."

"Yeah, lady," Graves added.

Liz, gritting teeth, glared at the mercenary. "First of all, it's *Doctor*, not lady…"

Graves shrugged. "Whatever you say, lady."

Susan's lip trembled, the back-and-forth in the room hammering on her already fried psyche. She realized the team was unaware of the real threat. Knowing the company, they probably gave some bullshit story about rebel units or smugglers in the rainforest. It was a miracle the team had made it this far without an encounter.

She looked to the leader, deciding he needed to be warned of what was really out here.

"Listen, Captain Ziler, right?" she said.

"Yes," he replied.

"Listen, there's something you must know," she said. "The specimens we were working on, they—"

"That's enough, Dr. Cabot," Liz said.

"No," Susan said. "They *need* to know."

Liz slapped leather. Susan immediately shut up, eyeing the hand resting on the Beretta. Even the mercenaries were caught off guard. This company bitch was willing to gun her staff member down right here in front of everybody.

"Whoa!" Graves swung his weapon in the doctor's direction.

"Relax," Ziler said, redirecting Graves' gun with his hand before turning his attention back to Liz. "Keep that hog skinned, Doc."

"I call the shots here, Captain," she said.

"That only goes so far," he replied. "But that doesn't mean I'll stand for you blowing holes in random civilians."

Liz kept her eyes on Susan, whose lips were zipped shut. The bruised, tired scientist had her hands partially raised, looking away as though she suspected this moment to be her last.

Slowly, Ziler put himself between her and Liz.

"I'm not burying your secret under human flesh," he said.

Liz watched the muzzle of his rifle. It was pointed toward the floor, ready to point in her direction in a flash. She would not outdraw him... especially with the shakes starting to reveal themselves again.

"Captain?" It was Medford's voice on the comm. He sounded both concerned and confused.

"Go ahead."

"Sir... there's some—something out here... I hear something..."

CHAPTER 9

The great beast fought with the strength of twenty men. It was the last of its family, the others having been claimed by the flying demons that now plagued this rainforest.

Weighing over four hundred pounds and standing at one-point-seven meters, the male mountain gorilla had nothing to lose. Its fight against the flying creatures was driven by vengeance as much as it was self-preservation. It had managed to slaughter two of them so far. The first was swatted out of the air, then pounded into the dirt with hammer-like fists. The second attempted to plunge its dagger of a mouth into its chest, but instead found itself in the primate's powerful grip. One hand grabbed it by the head, the other by the abdomen. The exoskeleton cracked, the internal guts stretching and splitting as the body was pulled apart.

Yet, the others kept coming. Unlike the gorilla, who was emotionally distraught by the death of its mate and brothers, these huge insects were completely unfazed by the loss of their companions. Instead, it was as though they were competing for blood rather than acting in unison.

They zipped around their target, the collective droning of their wings wreaking havoc on the gorilla's eardrums. The gorilla pivoted left and right, swatting angrily. The bugs were agile, evading its blows by mere inches. Frustration and fatigue began to weigh the primate down.

It set its sights on one of the bugs. Standing on its hind legs, the gorilla lunged. The bug ascended, avoiding the haymaker.

In that moment, one of the others seized the opportunity. It darted down and latched itself onto the primate's furry back, immediately plunging its probiscis into its shoulder.

The gorilla lurched backward, startled by pain. It fell and rolled repeatedly, clawing at the vermin with both hands. It found a wing and pulled, plucking the appendage off the attacker's body. It reached again, this time finding a leg. It yanked the limb free, its end dripping yellow fluid.

The bug seemed to take no notice, gorging on the gorilla's blood even while its own body was mutilated. Only when the primate body-slammed itself repeatedly into the forest floor did the insect finally lose its grip.

Righting itself, the gorilla turned to face its attacker, the needle-like mouthpart stained with its blood. Two fists crashed down, turning the four-foot-long body into mulch.

There was no victory in slaying the vermin. Its sisters converged on the primate's exposed back. Multiple daggers entered its body.

The gorilla reared its head back and roared, swatting blindly. As it did, other bugs attacked from the front, their mouths now piercing its chest and stomach. Covered in buzzing wings, the primate's strength was literally sucked from its body.

Overrun and overwhelmed, it collapsed. Gradually, its cries faded into silence. Meanwhile, its attackers' abdomens swelled with the fruits of their labor. Those who were not able to partake in the feeding were forced to move elsewhere.

Fortunately for them, new prey had arrived near the river—in the exact habitat where they were born. The bugs had no sentimentality. Only an urge to feed.

Eager to fulfill that urge, they converged on the new target.

***

The sudden silence in the forest was somehow worse than the assembly of dreadful howls that echoed moments before. Medford stood near the generators, his eyes and weapon pointed at the trees.

Descher and Browne heard it too. They stood near the radio tower, inching their way to the boat while keeping their weapons fixed on the forest.

When Medford first heard the chorus, it was a simple series of swaying branches and grunting. He figured maybe it was a couple of animals hunting, or maybe getting it on. It was the animal kingdom. Anything was possible.

Gradually, the movements intensified, peaking with that deafening howl. Worse than that was the steady droning sound. Whatever it was, it was not originating from ground level. His trained ears tracked the source to the canopy.

Medford did not consider himself an expert on rainforest life, but he knew this sound was not natural.

"Stand by. We're on our way out," Ziler said through his earpiece.

"Let's go," Descher said.

Medford turned to join the others, only to stop after two steps. The sound grew nearer, accompanied by the sound of thrashing leaves. He saw Ankrum on the boat, resting his M60 on the gunwale and angling it high.

"Heads up!"

Medford turned around and raised his F88 Austeyr, ready to spray bullets. He saw a mass of wings and outstretched legs closing in on him.

"CHRIST!!!"

He unleashed a burst, exploding the narrow center mass into a glob of shell and yellow-green guts. As the assailant hit the ground, its sisters followed. Medford backpedaled, fighting through the shock of witnessing this horrific foe. Despite their enormous size, there was no mistaking their shape and function.

Giant mosquitos, four feet in body length, had descended from the trees. Like a swarm of bees, they massed around the mercenary.

Overcome by shock and fright, the mercenary fired off several rounds. He turned to retreat, only to be cut off by more of the hovering insects. All at once, they closed in.

Large proboscises, eighteen inches in length, plunged into his neck, stomach, and thighs.

Yelling in agony, Medford was forced to the ground. The last thing he felt was the tightening of his flesh and the stiffening of his body as every drop of fluid was suctioned out of him.

Ziler tore through the front entrance and made a right turn, just in time to witness Medford go down.

"What in the name of…"

Now, it was clear what Dr. Cabot was about to inform him of. Out of the trees came a swarm of enormous mosquitos. Four of them were latched onto Medford's body, which was suddenly pasty white. The eyes imploded into their sockets, the screaming mouth stretching, the cheeks sinking between the jaws. Skeletal hands fell to the side.

"Medford!" Descher shouted. There was no way of getting a shot at the bugs without killing his friend. Not that it mattered in the long run.

The others followed Ziler out, each giving their own shocked reaction to seeing the swarm. There were at least two dozen of these mosquitos massing around Medford's corpse. Several of them branched out, interested in the other prey in the vicinity.

"Light 'em up," Ziler said.

Ankrum was way ahead of him. He pointed his M60 at the thickest congregation of bugs and depressed the trigger. A steady stream of ammunition entered the swarm. A soundtrack of gunfire and splattering insect bodies drummed across the research property. Machine gun bullets surgically cut through abdomens and thoraxes, removing their insides in an explosive display.

The bugs were unthreatened by the sound of gunfire and unfazed by the sight of their dead companions hitting the ground. They continued their assault, fanning out to herd the humans below.

Ziler centered one in his crosshairs. A single squeeze of the trigger brought the advancing mosquito to its end, its head disappearing in a messy greenish fountain.

Graves emptied his magazine into the swarm. Before reloading, he removed a grenade and pulled the pin. He counted down four of the five seconds he had before the ball was set to explode before tossing it skyward. The grenade went off, the shockwave and shrapnel driving the swarm apart.

Three mosquitos hit the ground. Graves reloaded his weapon and stood over the twitching body of an injured bug.

Bang!

Its head split open like a ripe melon, dumping brain matter onto the dirt.

The explosion only had momentary effect on the bugs. Several of them dove toward their prey, exposing their long mouthparts.

"Whoa!" Graves shouted. He and Wallington dove in separate directions, dodging an attack. The mosquito passed in-between them, immediately changing direction.

Wallington, now on his back, tracked the target with the muzzle of his weapon. A three-round burst put a round in all three segments of its body. The mosquito plummeted, its deflated body landing beside Graves.

"JES—" He flinched, looking at the dead thing lying beside him. Graves turned his eyes skyward, just in time to see another mosquito descending on him. "—SUS!"

He aimed his weapon high and fired. The mosquito's midsection exploded, its descent now a freefall. It landed directly on top of him.

"Shit! Shit! Shit! Shit! Shit!" Graves floundered, feeling the wetness of bug guts.

Ziler kicked the dead thing off of him, then proceeded to fend the swarm off with gunfire. No matter how many they killed, the damn things kept coming. There was no fear, no concern for safety. At most, they backed off for a split-second, only to resume the attack.

As he cut down another hostile, Ziler spotted one in his peripheral vision. It was swooping down, not toward him, but at Morales, who was preoccupied blasting at a small group converging near Ankrum.

The bug struck his back, driving him facedown against the dirt.

"Ah! AH! AHHHHH!" The mechanic writhed, feeling the edged claws digging at his back. Next, he yelled out as the probiscis plunged into his left shoulder. "GET IT OFF!" Ziler sprinted and kicked the mosquito's head as though it was a soccer ball. The bug reeled onto its back, wings and legs thrashing violently. He placed several rounds, ending its protest.

No sooner than the completion of the kill was he suddenly aware of an intense droning of wings directly above him. He looked up, just in time to see the bug before it tackled *him* to the ground.

"Mother—"

Ziler planted the frame of his weapon between himself and the creature's head, holding the tip of its proboscis from his neck by an inch.

Wallington and Graves came to the rescue, the former pressing the muzzle of his rifle to the left side of the bug's head. After a deafening gunshot, everything inside that head splattered through the exit wound.

Ziler and Morales stood up, only to retreat as several bugs converged on them.

In that moment, the cover fire ceased. With several bugs descending on him, Ankrum was forced to take cover in the deckhouse, blasting away with his G36. Without the machine gun support, the swarm's attack intensified.

Ziler had to make a split-second judgment. On the one hand, if they retreated into the building, the bugs would simply follow them inside. They'd be stuck in confined quarters, with too many points of entry to cover. On the other hand, being out in the open in this circumstance left them incredibly vulnerable to the mosquito attack.

"Get inside!" Ziler said. "Go! Go! Get in the building and take position in the main hall. We can bottleneck the bugs in there."

Graves and Wallington helped Morales into the building, with Susan right behind them. Liz was already at the door, firing a few shots from her Beretta before going inside.

Ziler arrived at the doorway, providing cover fire for Browne and Descher. Browne sprinted for the building, whilst the latter had retreated westward beyond the garage to avoid the swarm.

With many of the humans inside the habitat, many of the bugs converged on the clumsy, isolated member of the team.

"Descher!" Ziler shouted. "Move! Move! Move!"

The merc yelled out, his magazine now dry. Every which way he turned, the bugs were right there. He scampered left, right, forward, backward… each motion holding off his fate by mere seconds. Quivering hands found a fresh magazine and loaded it into his SA80.

He pointed the gun up and squeezed the trigger. The shots came too late. The bugs closed in around him, securing a grip with their feet. Like wooden stakes plunging into dirt, their mouths penetrated his flesh. Pain and panic put Descher's mind into a spiral. He fell to the ground, his weapon inadvertently pointing toward the tower.

Several rounds spat from its barrel.

As Ziler attempted to shoot the attackers, his ears picked up the sounds of bullets striking metal. He followed the direction of Descher's SA80 to the collection of fuel barrels near the tower.

He had no choice but to dive for cover.

BOOM!

A spark ignited the gas, which erupted into a tremendous explosion. A ball of fire consumed the lower portion of the tower, the shockwave pushing it toward the river. The south legs groaned, unable to support the tower's weight and tilt. The tower crashed into the river, its metal body briefly obscured by the large swell.

Ziler crouched in the lobby, ready to blast any bugs that dared to come through that window.

The swarm descended into chaos. The smoke and fire spread across the yard, engulfing the garage. Like a raging flood, the flames swept toward the generator…and the two fuel barrels between it and the facility.

He hurried into the hallway. "Move to the east end of the building! *Now!*"

Without hesitation, the mercenaries retreated the length of the hall, taking a right across from Lab Room Three. They entered the kitchen area right as the barrels exploded.

The building shook as a portion of the west wall imploded into Lab Rooms One and Two. Smoke and heat quickly filled the rest of the building.

The team formed firing lines in the kitchen, taking aim at the doorway and east window. There they remained, listening to the sound of buzzing wings as the mosquitos retreated into the rainforest.

CHAPTER 10

The buzzing of wings persisted for several minutes, gradually dying down as the bugs were repelled by the heat and thick smoke. Silence followed, broken after a few moments by Ankrum's voice through their earpieces.

"We're clear, Captain. The bastards have retreated."

"Copy that," Ziler said. He directed his team out the door. They stepped out into a smoke-filled hallway, forcing them to hold their breaths as they made their way outside.

Labs One and Two had practically imploded, their ceilings collapsing in on the workstations. Large portions of the west wall in both rooms were gone, giving free access to fire and smoke.

They hurried down the hall, feeling another wave of heat as they passed through the lounge area.

Outside, they found a wall of black towering over the facility. At the base of this tower of smoke were orange flames which ate away at the greenhouse, garage, and generators.

"There's extinguishers inside," Susan said, pointing back at the lounge.

Ziler and Wallington hurried inside and found the panel on the east wall. Even under these circumstances, the last thing anyone wanted to risk was a forest fire. With no rain on the horizon, the flames could easily spread and wipe out hundreds of acres before it could be stopped.

The two mercenaries dispersed the chemical agent onto the flames, halting their spread.

With the fire extinguished, the smoke gradually began to thin. Ziler tossed the spent fire extinguisher aside, then slowly approached the fallen radio tower. It had fallen directly across the river, cutting them off.

"We've got problems," Ankrum said, observing the aftermath from the flying bridge. "No way we're gonna be able to move that thing."

"Can't stay here," Ziler said. "Hiding in the research building is a death trap at this point. It's only a matter of time before those things come back."

"So…" Graves scratched the back of his head. "…Are we just gonna pretend that was a normal occurrence? Giant fucking mosquitos?" He hit Dr. Liz Moore with a fierce stare. "Time for an explanation, Doctor."

Liz shook her head. "It must be a byproduct of—"

"Byproduct, my ass, Doctor," Graves said.

Liz looked to Ziler, pointing her thumb at Graves. "Control your dog, Captain."

"Nah." Ziler shook his head. "Two of our men are dead…"

"Nearly three," Morales said, wincing as Wallington applied disinfectant and a dressing to the stab wound in his shoulder.

"Explanation time, Doctor Moore," Ziler said.

"You aren't paid to ask questions. You're paid to follow orders and complete the assignment," Liz snapped. Her face was beet red, aside from two purple veins stretching the length of her forehead. "Right now, your job is to get us back to the extraction site."

"Ankrum's already looking over the map," Ziler said. "And to complete the job, it's best I know exactly what I'm up against."

"Well... you saw them, didn't you?" Liz said, waving her hand at the sky.

Ziler groaned. "Dr. Cabot. Mind sharing what you were about to disclose before we were... let's say, rudely interrupted?"

Susan glanced nervously in Liz's direction.

"Don't worry about her," Ziler said.

Liz shook her head. "It's not any of their business. These are company secrets, Dr. Cabot. You speak... you can rest assured you'll never work again in your life."

Twenty minutes ago, that threat would have had a lot of weight. Now, all Susan cared about was her own survival, as well as that of these men who were helping. Though she would not necessarily describe them as angels, they were definitely not monsters. Already, they had lost two men thanks to the company's experimentation. They deserved to know the whole truth.

"As you saw, those were giant mosquitos," she said. "When I was sent out here, I was under the impression I was going to be developing new vaccines for a variety of severe illnesses. Instead, I was developing vaccines for viruses that didn't even exist yet... until our lab created them..."

"You filthy..." Liz gripped her pistol.

Ziler nodded at Graves, who eagerly moved in. He grabbed the doctor by the wrist, twisting it behind her back.

"Hey!" she squealed.

"Let go, Ms. Doctor," Graves said. "Don't prolong this too much. I might get curious as to what's in your back pocket."

Cursing, Liz conceded. The mercenary took her pistol and released her arm, pleased with himself, having successfully gotten under her skin. Liz clenched her jaw, tempted to throw a barrage of insults at the band of mercenaries. Ultimately, she stayed silent. An outburst would only satisfy Graves all the more. Taking a deep breath, she bit her tongue while Susan Cabot continued explaining the research team's true purpose.

Susan took a few steps in Ziler's direction, seeing him as her protector, not only against giant mutated bugs, but the crazed scientist.

"I, uh…"

"Relax, Dr. Cabot," Ziler said. "Explain everything."

"Right," she said. "It probably comes as no surprise to all of you that there's a lot of money in pharmaceuticals. Medicine only works when there's a specific illness for it to counteract. When there's a *new* illness, such as a fast-spreading virus, the demand for a vaccine will be off the charts…"

"Give us the short version, Doctor," Ziler said. "So, the company sent you here to make the vaccine for a whole new virus. Is that virus made from *mosquitos*, by any chance?"

Susan nodded. "That's correct." She looked at Liz. "The plan was to somehow disperse the virus onto various parts of the world, cast blame on some country or group, then come out looking like the heroes. 'Look here. We've developed a new vaccine in record time!'"

"So you got the viruses from mosquitos?" Wallington said.

"Not *I,*" Susan said. "There were two teams, one specifically for extracting the virus from the bugs and developing methods to disperse them. I was developing the vaccine." She gave another look in Liz's direction. "And I never would have taken part, had I known the truth."

"Sure you would have, Doctor," Liz retorted. "Why, you practically came crawling to us. With your background, nobody was ever going to hire you. Not even with your brilliant mind. The way I see it, if not for

Lexington, you'd be working the street corner at night, if you know what I mean…"

"Listen, bitch…"

"Alright, alright, alright," Wallington said, stepping in-between them. "Okay, Dr. Cabot… I understand what you're saying, but what I don't understand is why make the mosquitos giant sized. What's the purpose of that?"

"And how?" Graves added.

"Simple," Susan said. "They developed a growth hormone. I'm assuming you met Jorge."

"Big fella? A little furry? Big long tail?" Graves said in his usual snarky tone. "Bit of an attitude problem?"

"Yep, that's him," Susan said. "It's hard to apply the growth hormone to insects as small as mosquitos, so they enlarged some rats first. The mosquitos fed off Jorge's blood and voila, they ingested the growth hormone. Over time, they and their larva began to enlarge."

"Let me guess," Graves put a finger to his chin, pretending to think hard. "Some of them escaped."

"There was an accident," Susan said. "Jorge went nuts. Broke a container of freshly dosed mosquitos. Needless to say, they escaped. We tried to track them down, but after a while, we assumed they escaped through the vents."

"How small were they?" Wallington asked.

"Maybe the size of a flash card," Susan said. "A couple weeks later, one of the guys reported seeing one somewhere down the river. We tried to report it, but Liz did not relay the call. 'Too close to the deadline,' I recall her saying on the radio. That was a week ago. Fast-forward to yesterday…" Susan took a deep breath as a montage of horrible memories zipped through her mind. "They hit us hard out of nowhere. One minute, we were just following our daily routines, then WHAM!

Mosquitos *everywhere!* Dr. Aaron pushed me into the cellar and ran to the radio room to make a call."

Morales walked to the edge of the shore, longingly watching the west stretch on the other side of the fallen tower.

"So, the growth hormone can be passed into another body through consumption?" he asked.

"Correct," Susan said.

"That explains that big fish we encountered," he said. "A couple of those bugs probably lingered too close to the water. Got grabbed by that fish. Next thing he knows, he's the size of a boat."

"How many were in that container?" Ziler asked.

"Maybe twenty?" Susan replied.

Ziler clenched his teeth. "There were way more than twenty in that swarm." He looked at the thick forest that surrounded him and his team. "They've made a nest somewhere. Spawned other mutant mosquitos, who in turn are probably laying new eggs. Bugs that size don't have any natural predators."

"These species hatch a few days once the eggs are lain," Susan added. "A single mosquito can lay a hundred eggs at a time."

Graves turned pale. "For real?"

"They'll overrun this entire rainforest in a month," Ziler said. He watched Liz, who appeared to inch away from the group as the conversation went on. She had her arms crossed, her face still pulsing with irritation. "Problem there, Dr. Moore?"

"You know my superiors will learn about this conversation as soon as we return," she said.

"Yeah, as will the authorities, as much as it pains me to say it," Ziler replied. "You do realize the magnitude of this situation, right? This outbreak is not going to be limited to the Congo Rainforest. They'll branch out and invade all of Africa, then the rest of the world. Before long, there'll be no way of stopping them. Don't think any vaccine will come in handy when your blood's literally being drained from your body."

"How 'bout you just worry about getting us back home?" Liz said. "Once we're in the air, I'll use the satellite phone to make a call to Jed Pervis. He'll get it taken care of by the end of the week."

Ziler snorted. "Best of luck with that."

Liz took a step in his direction, shoulders squared. "Listen, Captain—"

"So, Ankrum," he said, ignoring the doctor. He boarded the boat and stood alongside the gunner, observing the river map. "What's our route looking like?"

Ankrum traced his finger along the thin blue line, stopping at a fork that broke off to the south. "Our best bet is to take this little detour. It'll take us south about a mile, then it hooks back to the west. Thank God for small favors, this will essentially take us back to the rendezvous point. We'll miss it by a few miles, but there's a little branch over here to the west we can use to circle back to where we arrived."

"Good. How's the boat?"

"Took a bit of shrapnel during the crash, but still functional," Ankrum said.

"Maybe we should just have the chopper come here," Liz said.

"Look above you," Ziler said. Liz muttered something under her breath, then looked at the thick canopy above them. The upper layers of canopy branched out, almost completely covering the clearing.

"All that money spent building this place, and Lexington couldn't bother to do some basic tree trimming," Graves said.

"That post down the river was already stationed there," Liz said. "We bought it and decided to take advantage of the unique spot. Sorry we didn't anticipate a giant bug invasion."

"Oh, that's easy," Graves said. "When you're engineering giant mosquitos in the middle of the jungle, it's not a stretch to assume things might go wrong. Especially when you have people with certain 'habits' running the show."

"Pardon me?" Liz said.

Grave snickered. "Like you don't know what I'm talking about."

"Everyone, get aboard," Ziler said. "Let's get the hell out of here before those things come back. Dr. Moore, I just ask you keep your distance from Dr. Cabot during our trip."

Liz held back, waiting for the other mercenaries to board the vessel. She pulled the altoids from her pocket, tossed a couple in her mouth, then stepped aboard.

The not-so-subtle shaking of the container was noticed by everyone as she disappeared into the deckhouse.

CHAPTER 11

It was a tense and quiet boat ride. Two miles upriver, they reached the fork. Ziler took the right as though steering a truck off the highway. All eyes were on the surrounding forest. Tall trees leaned over the river, appearing to taunt them with their thick vegetation. There was no field of view past fifty feet. Seventy, if they were very lucky.

Every time a bird flew overhead, the team tensed up.

"They have a distinct sound," Ziler reminded them, his second cigar rocking between his teeth. "Buzzing wings and flapping wings are way different. Use your ears, people."

They continued following the bend. After roughly two-thirds of a mile, they were now heading westward.

There was eight miles to go before they reached their destination. With some luck, they would be back at the rendezvous point sometime that afternoon. All they could do for now was to keep alert and pray not to encounter those bugs.

Susan stood near the flying bridge in total silence. It was clear the mercenaries were not in the mood for chatter. They had taken defensive positions on the boat, each one looking as though they were patrolling a river during the Vietnam War. In a sense, they really were at war. Already, two of their squad members had met a horrific end. To make matters worse, they were fighting an enemy with hardly any fear of death.

The relative lack of animal life made things even more daunting. By now, they should've seen an abundance of fauna. Leopards, primates, aardvarks. Yet, there was hardly anything.

Even worse were the empty huts. In the many months of working here, there had been some sightings of rainforest dwellers. Their homes, set within areas clear of undergrowth, generally resembled wooden igloos, with a frame constructed with saplings and walls made from shingled tree leaves.

As the team passed the homes, they could not spot one single inhabitant. The horrid smell, which permeated the area around the laboratory, was present here. It was clear and present evidence that the bugs were branching out throughout the rainforest.

Susan's stomach churned. Not only had the experiment claimed the lives of her colleagues, it had claimed those of innocent locals. Lexington wasn't invited here, nor did it own any stake in the land. They simply moved in, took what they wanted, bribed who they needed to, not giving a damn who got hurt in the process.

The silence continued for the next mile. By then, the smell had dissipated, though the ghosts of the rainforest still haunted Susan's thoughts.

Liz stood across from her, noticeably eyeing the deckhouse entrance. Her hand kept going to her empty holster. Other times, it was to her back pocket, then to the pouch in her vest where she kept her thumb drive.

Susan noticed something else in that pouch... something that managed to reflect sunlight. Glass vials.

She got the samples.

Liz noticed the virologist eyeballing her. "Got a problem?"

"Can I have a word with you?" Susan asked.

"When we get back to camp," Liz said. Her fingers tapped the guardrail, their rhythm gradually picking up speed until, finally, Liz went for the door. "I'll be back in a moment."

Susan heard Graves snort, then mutter something under his breath. She could not help but suspect he knew something she didn't. Was Liz making a phone call? She had that SAT phone. Was she making a call to the company to discuss what to do with the troublesome Dr. Susan Cabot? After all, she was willing to shoot her in front of all of these mercenaries. If anything, that indicated Susan wasn't long for this world if the company had any say-so.

No way was she going to wait until they returned to the site in Cameroon. Susan marched into the deckhouse, expecting to see Liz on the phone.

Instead, Liz was leaning over the galley table. She looked back suddenly, shocked to see Dr. Cabot walking in on her.

"The hell?" She looked down to the table and began rolling something up in what sounded like thin plastic. "What are you doing in here?"

"Didn't realize the galley was off limits," Susan said. "The hell are you doing?"

"Nothing."

Susan marched to the table, seeing the brown powder being rolled up into a ball. "Yep… 'nothing'. Right."

"It's just a—"

"Oh, shut up," Susan said. The SAT phone was sticking out of a vest pocket. "Mind if I take that? I'd like to make a call."

"Maybe later," Liz said.

"No, I'd like to do it now."

Liz turned to square up with her. "I said later."

Susan kicked the leg of the table. The heroin baggie unraveled, threatening to spill its contents onto the deck.

Liz gasped, lunging for her stash to keep it from scattering. While both of her hands were frantically occupied, Susan took the opportunity to reach into Liz's vest.

"The hell are you doing?!" Liz shouted, trying to fight the virologist off while simultaneously protecting her stash.

"Taking... this!" Susan yanked the phone free, quickly turning her back.

Liz turned around, ready to throw hands. "You fucking crazy bitch..."

The door flung open. Wallington and Graves stepped inside.

"The hell's going on in here?" the medic said.

"Catfight?" Graves said.

Liz quickly turned around to obscure the drugs on the table. "Get out of here, will ya?"

"Why?" Graves said, grinning.

"Not now, man," Wallington said. He looked to Susan. "You all right?"

She nodded. "Yeah. Just having a little... disagreement." She held up the phone.

"Gotchya," he replied. "I'll... stay right outside the door in case there are other 'disagreements'."

The two mercenaries stepped outside, leaving the two women by themselves.

Liz stuffed her stash into her back pocket.

Susan shook her head. "Guess the rumors were true."

"What rumors?" Liz said, her voice a low growl.

"Oh, just stuff flying around the camp about Dr. Moore and her little habit," Susan said. "Some say it's why you took this job, because it gave you fairly easy access to suppliers without the DEA being on your back. So, when'd you start? During your service? Some of that stuff floats around the Middle East."

"Not important," Liz said. "We all have our vices, Doctor. And our flaws. I know you have yours. Why else would you have taken the job with my company?"

Susan's eyes hit the floor. She should have known Liz would bring up her past. In her case, her own vices led to the mistake that would define her life. That downward spiral of bad decisions led her here, under the guise of bettering humanity. As it turned out, she was just playing a role in some CEO's scheme to inflate his pockets with cash.

"You wanna kill yourself with that stuff? Fine. You do you," she said. "My concern is my own safety. I don't wanna get suicided so some company secrets can remain buried."

"Fine," Liz said. "Then sign an NDA. I'll arrange it with the bosses."

Susan swallowed, tempted to say yes to that offer. At least there was a glimmer of hope she would be able to live her life without fear of retaliation. Then again, these were just words. Empty, meaningless words without action to back them up.

"What about the vaccine development project? Are they still planning to continue with that?"

"What's it matter to you?" Liz said.

"It matters because it's wrong," Susan said.

Liz chuckled. "Wrong? What's 'wrong' about it? This is the way things are. What? You believe the world runs on some moral code? That people do the things they do because they're virtuous? You think every illness that exists came into the world naturally? You think companies, like Lexington, create products because they're run by good and decent human beings? You must be the type who believes the 'freedom' narrative when countries invade each other. Certainly, there's no money being made there... right?"

Liz took a breath, then stuffed her drugs into her back pocket. "That's the way of the world, Dr. Cabot. Either get on board or get the hell out of the way."

"Or be forced out of the way?" Susan said.

Liz shrugged nonchalantly. "It if comes to that." She held out her hand, nodding towards the satellite phone. "If you are willing to get off your high horse, I might be able to keep you in the company. We're always in need of doctors and researchers."

Susan looked at Liz's hand, then at her phone. "Or… maybe I can call every major news agency there is and inform them of Lexington's illegal activities." She held up the phone, daring Liz to take a swipe at it.

The company liaison stared at her with pin-point pupils, her movements a tad sluggish after her latest fix. At this moment, Susan realized Liz was a bit skinnier than when she had last seen her. Liz's habits had definitely worsened in the past several months, to the point where she needed multiple fixes a day.

If there was anything Susan understood, it was that company people and drug addicts practically lied through their teeth for a living. Liz Moore was both. Any deal she offered to Susan needed to be taken with a grain—or rather, a cup—of salt.

Susan backed toward the door. "I'll hang on to this." Liz remained in place, looking at the window, rather than at Susan herself. Out the door she went, holding the phone as though it was a block of nitro.

When she turned around, she saw what Liz was really watching.

"Oh! Mr. Ziler," she said. "Excuse me. *Captain* Ziler."

He stood with his arms crossed, waiting for the door to swing shut. It was no mystery why he was standing right outside the deckhouse, listening in. There wasn't a molecule of trust for Liz Moore on this boat, especially after the altercation in Lab Room Three.

"It's just a habit. I met most of these guys while I was on active duty. Come on." He gestured to the flying bridge. "Let's head up there, shall we?"

They climbed to the flying bridge, where Wallington now stood after trading places with Ziler.

"Everything good downstairs, Cap?"

"As fine as eating spicy food when you have a stomach ulcer," Ziler replied. He reclaimed his spot at the helm and returned his cigar to his lips. Susan stood beside him, her arms wrapped around her middle as she idly watched the trees passing by. She had not quite gotten over the intense events at the facility.

"You'll be fine, Doctor," Wallington said. "We'll get you out of here."

"I appreciate it," she said. "You guys can call me Susan, by the way."

"Alright, Susan," Ziler said.

"I just realized I never thanked you for everything you did back there at the lab," she said. "Getting me out of there, keeping Dr. Moore in check…"

"I see you've got her SAT phone," Ziler said.

"I was thinking about making a few calls," Susan said. "There were some corrupt people who worked in that lab, *but* there were many good people as well. People who felt they had no other choice but to work for that company, or were duped into believing they were working on a good cause."

"Was that what happened to you?" Ziler said. "How'd someone like you get involved in this?"

Susan leaned on the console and exhaled sharply. It wasn't a story she was eager to share. However, these men had saved her life twice already, and by the looks of it, were willing to keep her safe from the company if necessary. If anyone deserved to know the truth, it was them.

"A combination of bad decisions and gullibility," she said.

Ziler knew what she was implying. He nodded, keeping his eyes on the river ahead of them.

"Let me guess," he said. "You got into some trouble in a past job, which wrecked your place in the job market, despite having exceptional skill in your field. Along comes Lexington, who offers you a unique position developing a new vaccine which 'could save millions'. Am I close?"

"Pretty much nailed it to a tee," Susan said. "I guess you know Lexington all too well."

"I know people all too well," Ziler said. "Some are bad, others are good, but get desperate. They feel like they have no options. In some cases, they are willing to do things they wouldn't normally do."

"Right is still right and wrong is still wrong," Susan said. "Everything I've done is wrong. Before Lexington, I was developing a new single-dose treatment for malaria. Long story short, I pushed it hard, despite my associates claiming it was not ready. I was sure it would work, so I tested it on some patients. As a result, the medication caused the platelets to attack the red blood cells. Their bodies became war zones. Five patients died before we could counteract the effects." She shut her eyes. "Needless to say, I lost everything. My license, funding, marriage... *everything*. Now, here I am, in another mess."

"Maybe," Wallington said.

"'Maybe'?" Susan said, chuckling. "I am. There's no 'maybe' about it."

"Okay, so you're in another jam," he said. "But this was going to happen with or without you. Maybe I believe too much in fate, but maybe your journey has led you to this—for you to be the one that'll *stop* a manmade pandemic."

She looked at the phone. "That's one way of looking at it. Assuming I even live long enough to get word out. I'm surprised you're so supportive, seeing that Lexington is your client."

Ziler shrugged. "I doubt they'll be hiring us after this, anyway."

That got a smile from Susan. Maybe it was from watching movies, but she naturally thought of mercenaries as guns-for-hire, lacking in morality, willing to do anything as long as the pay was right. While that was likely true for some contractors, that stereotype was not representative of these guys.

Thank God it was this team that was sent...

"I need to take a leak," Graves announced. "How far you think I can shoot it out?"

Susan smirked.

...as obnoxious as some of them are.

Ankrum shook his head. "Hard to say. You know the general rule: the smaller the weapon, the shorter the range."

The other mercs laughed at Graves' expense.

"Oh, ha-ha." He flipped the bird and unzipped his fly. Standing over the bow, he let it rip. "Ahhhhh. Look at that."

"No... I'd rather not," Morales said.

"Same here," Wallington added. He turned his back, glancing at Susan. "You're lucky. We have to *live* with that."

Graves finished up firing his golden stream, then zipped back up. He turned around with a juvenile look of pride on his face.

"I'd say that was a good twelve feet."

"More like five feet," Morales said.

"Oh, shut up," Graves said. He pointed at a few branches protruding from the water a few feet from the shoreline. "If I wanted to, I could've showered those twigs. Or hell, I could've reached the shore. Maybe could've drenched those... whatever those are." He pointed at a spot farther west on the shoreline. Up ahead to the right was a cove with what appeared to be vegetation. Vines, moss, and other green buildup stood high, resembling tall structural figures. For a moment, it appeared as though they had stumbled upon some kind of ancient temple.

"I'm sure you could," said a very disinterested Ankrum.

"The hell are those?" Morales said. "Doesn't look like trees."

Everyone else turned their attention to the oddity. Ziler slowed the boat down, trying to figure out what he was looking at. He gently steered it left, bringing them within twenty feet of the shore.

Then he saw the mast and the rusted metal that made up the prow. They were looking at an old, abandoned supply boat. On the shore beyond it were a pair of broken-down wooden buildings. These structures were not huts, but far larger, comprising of at least two-thousand square feet.

As they drew near, they detected the smell of rusted steel. Near the rotted structures were steel crates, sealed shut and covered in vegetation. The boat itself was all brown, as opposed to its original gray color. The windows were broken, the props crammed against weeds in the shallows.

"Oh, my lord," Susan said. "I never knew this was here. What is this?"

Ziler pointed to the bow of the vessel. "See that? German lettering. What's left of it, anyway."

"What's a German boat doing all the way out here?" Wallington said.

Ziler stopped the boat and used his binoculars to visually comb through the area. Near one of the crates was something that resembled a long stick. He would have assumed that's what it was, had it not been for the stock and the bolt action.

"Gewehr 98s," he said.

"Guns?" Graves said.

"Old ass guns," Ankrum added.

"As in... a hundred years old," Ziler said. "I think this was a German camp from World War One. It's probably a communications camp, set up during the African Theatre of the First World War. That's my guess, anyway."

"Looks like they left a lot of shit behind," Susan said.

"Yeah, probably had to leave in a hurry," Ziler said. "If I had to speculate further, it was probably evacuated during the string of conflicts that led to the capture of Douala in Cameroon."

"Who's Douala?" Graves said.

"Not a person, genius. It's a place," Wallington said.

"Well excuuuuuse me," Graves muttered.

Ziler eased on the throttle, putting the camp behind them. It was a neat, obscure piece of history from a lesser-known aspect of World War One. Still, its significance paled to their survival.

Ankrum took a breath, maintaining a fierce grip on his M60.

"Still quiet. So far, so good."

Graves nudged him with his foot. "Better not have jinxed us..."

CHAPTER 12

"Goddamnit, Ankrum! You fucking jinxed us!"

The silent trip had turned loud with buzzing wings and rapid gunfire. They came out of the trees in a massive swarm. Dozens of mutated insects hovered over the boat, thirsty for human blood.

Graves was the first to open fire, cursing as he attempted to repel the swarm. The damn things would not hold still, nor did they keep a consistent pattern of flight.

Ziler shouldered his weapon. "Dr. Cabot, take the helm." He traded places with her and began blasting away. His first shots were on point, his target spiraling into the water, trailing green blood.

Its brethren took no notice of their fallen member. Compassion, remorse, and fear were not in their DNA code. The bugs were like machines, focused on a single goal.

Browne and Morales took position on the starboard side, ducking repeatedly as mosquitos dove at them. On the front of the vessel, Ankrum had his M60 aimed over the port bow, blasting into the patch of trees where the bugs came from. His barrage of bullets cut down a few of them on their way out, but failed to repel the others.

Susan gunned the throttle in hopes of outrunning the swarm. Through the fog of fluttering wings and bright muzzle flashes, she watched the river. Up ahead was a fork to the left, leading into an area with thick canopy.

"Want me to take a left?!" she shouted to Ziler.

All of a sudden, Liz was sprinting up to the flying bridge. "No! No! No!" That leads to a cove. We'd be trapped. Here!" She pushed Susan out of the way. "Let me handle this. You're clearly not experienced with boats."

Susan didn't bother arguing. Even if she wanted to, it would have been impossible, as a mosquito swooped down on top of her. Susan screamed, falling down the short flight of steps onto the main deck. The mosquito positioned itself on her back, ready to plunge its probiscis into her meat.

Instead, it was the bug itself that suffered a fatal penetration. The silent Browne sprinted across the deck, his buck knife in hand. The blade pierced the exoskeleton with ease, the silver blade painted green with the insect's blood.

The masked mercenary lifted the dying mosquito off of the doctor, its legs still flailing. Browne unsheathed one of his push-daggers and rammed the arrow-shaped blade into its head. The bug spasmed, then went limp.

Browne flung its corpse into the water, then unslung his weapon to resume firing.

Wallington hurried to the main deck and helped Susan to her feet.

"You all right?"

"Yeah, I'm fi—"

They both ducked as another mosquito made a run at them.

"Shit!" Wallington pivoted left and fired several shots over the port quarter. The mosquito never knew what hit it. Its back opened up, showering its insides onto the river. The bug plummeted, vanishing behind a tremendous splash.

As the battle raged on, Liz kept the boat going at top speed, passing the cove on the left side.

"Jesus, they're everywhere," Morales said.

Fed up with the swarming over his head, Ankrum pointed his M60 straight into the air. Steadying the weapon with bulking arms, he began spraying the swarm.

Splat! Splat! Splat!

One of their bodies spattered on the deck right in front of Susan, making her jump back.

Ankrum continued firing, his weapon devouring the ammo belt and spitting the empty casing onto the deck. Once the machine gun ran empty, he discarded it and plucked a pair of grenades from his vest. Remembering Graves' daring tactic during their previous encounter with the bugs, he pulled the pins, released the striker levers, then launched the two grenades high over the starboard side.

Two simultaneous explosions resulted in a concussion blast, dropping multiple mosquitos.

Morales, watching as dead bugs rained down, decided to give it a try. He slung his M4 Carbine over his shoulder, its mag having run dry. He yanked a grenade from his chest, pulled the pin, reached back to throw it at a group of bugs several meters off the port quarter...

The sound of buzzing wings filled his ears. He glanced over his shoulder, just in time to see the mosquito bearing down on him.

For the second time that day, he felt the plunge of a proboscis, this time in the back of his neck. Yelling in agony, the mechanic was forced facedown onto the deck, his attacker wasting no time in suctioning the blood from his body.

The grenade rolled from his grip... directly toward Susan and Wallington. The medic saw the striker lever fling from the ball. In five seconds, they would be peppered with shrapnel. There was no cover, nowhere to go... except into the water.

"Geez—" Wallington grabbed Susan and threw her, and himself over the side. At the same time, Browne, Ankrum, and Graves dove for cover on the bow.

The grenade detonated, imploding Morales' face, and shattering a large section of the main deck.

The concussion from the blast reached all of the remaining team members, resulting in ringing ears and warped vision.

Ziler stood up, having ducked with Liz behind the control console. When he looked up, he saw a large smoking gap in the deck, and a dead Morales—his face and shoulders crunched inward, his skin pasty white.

Wallington and Susan were not there.

Hearing the sound of splashing, Ziler looked over his shoulder. Wallington and Susan were several yards behind them, struggling for dear life as a small band of mosquitos hovered over them.

"Dr. Moore. Turn the boat around," he said. "We've got people overboard."

"Nothing we can do for them," Liz said.

"Damn it, Doctor, turn this boat around, or…"

Three mosquitos descended on him, forcing him to abandon his threat. Ziler fired his weapon, killing one of the bugs. The other two closed in, legs outstretched, their proboscises ready to stab him.

Ziler thrust the butt of his weapon outward, knocking the nearest mosquito out of the air. The second one charged at full force, ramming him against Liz and the console.

Liz screamed, feeling the wings slapping against her face.

Ziler, his back against the helm, drew his sidearm and pressed the muzzle to the mosquito's head.

Bang!

The creature's head split open, its life abruptly ceasing.

Ziler kicked the fresh corpse aside and reloaded his rifle. As he slammed the magazine in place, his nose picked up the scent of smoke. He heard the grinding of gears, as well as a sharp, pecking sound.

Peeking over the stern, he realized their problems were worsening. Two mosquitos, likely drawn by the vibration, attacked the outboard prop. Sparks flew, the engine spitting smoke.

He put several rounds into the two insects. Their limp bodies splashed into the water, one of them getting chopped by the propellors.

The damage was done. The motor had been penetrated by their mouthparts, the internal components compromised.

Already, the boat was slowing down.

"The hell's going on?" Liz said. She looked back and saw the damaged motor. "Oh, shit."

"There's no choice," Ziler said. "Get us to shore."

"And be trapped in the forest?" Liz said.

"Doctor, we're almost dead in the water," Ziler said.

"Cap!" Graves shouted. After firing off a few shots at some passing mosquitos, he pointed to his ten o'clock. "Huts!"

Ziler followed his finger, spotting the small wooden structure. He wasn't thrilled about holing up in a house made of branches and leaves, but at this point, he didn't have any better alternatives.

"Take us there."

Liz turned the boat to port. The engine sputtered, the prop completing a few final rotations before coming to a stop. The boat had just enough momentum to take them all the way to shore.

Meanwhile, the swarm kept pace with the boat.

The three mercenaries on the main deck spread out, waiting for their moment to abandon ship.

Seven feet from shore, the boat ran aground.

"Let's go!" Ziler shouted. He and Liz leapt from the flying bridge into the edge of the river, landing in three feet of water. As soon as they touched down, they sprinted inland, straight for the abandoned hut.

Graves was first off the bow, followed by Browne.

Ankrum provided cover fire, successfully cutting down a couple of mosquitos with his G36.

"How ya like that?" he said.

Ziler reached the hut, pushing Liz through the entryway. He turned around, waving for the others to hurry up.

"Ankrum! Get your ass over here—above you!" He raised his M27, exploding the head of a mosquito that hovered above the heavy gunner.

Ankrum leapt from the boat. In that moment, two mosquitos charged, slamming into him in midair. Ankrum yelled out, having lost his center of gravity. He landed on his back, briefly submerged in water. He emerged and frantically crawled ashore.

Ziler continued popping off rounds, desperately trying to keep the bugs off of his mercenary. He was forced to redirect his aim as a group of mosquitos closed in from his three o'clock.

He backed into the hut, gunning the bugs down one-by-one as they attempted to follow him inside.

"Ah! AHHH!"

Ziler hurried back outside, just in time to see the bugs swarm Ankrum. The gunner drew his pistol and fired several rounds into the horde, most of his shots missing entirely.

A mass of buzzing wings encompassed him. In the blink of an eye, all of Ankrum's tactical training had vanished. He descended into a flurry of panicked kicking and screaming, then arched back as multiple bugs penetrated his flesh.

His screams took on a gargling sound. His tongue protruded between his teeth, shriveling into a dark thing that resembled a snake's tail. His flesh hugged his skeleton, the skin rapidly losing its color.

At the same time, his attackers' bodies swelled, their abdomens taking on a bright pinkish color.

"Damn it!" Ziler backed into the hut. Unfortunately, there was no door to shut. Immediately, multiple insects converged on the entrance.

The team repelled them with a flurry of rifle fire. Bullet impacts tore into the bugs, who were seemingly replaced immediately by new members.

Graves reloaded his rifle, listening to the buzzing of wings outside the west wall.

"Might be a good time to come up with a plan," he said. "I only have a couple magazines left."

"Hang on," Ziler said.

Browne switched places with him, taking firing position in front of the entryway. His M4 Carbine successfully prevented another mosquito from infiltrating the hut.

The sound of scraping on the ceiling made them look up. The mosquitos were on the roof, jabbing their proboscises through the leaf shingles. Slowly but truly, they were widening the space between the branches.

"Hope you're thinking fast, Captain," Graves said.

"Just... hold on."

It wasn't often when Ziler was short on ideas. Going outside was suicide, yet so was staying in here. Returning to the boat was useless. The mosquitos were not repelled by gunfire. They would simply attack again and again until their prey was overwhelmed.

The only thing that did successfully repel the bugs was fire and smoke.

He looked to the boat, and the two fuel drums that rested on the forward deck.

"Browne, mind if I borrow that Bowie knife?"

Browne unsheathed the monster of a knife and handed it over, his eyes conveying his unspoken question. *The hell do you have in mind?*

"Cover me," Ziler said.

"Cover…" Before Graves could protest, Ziler was out the door. The two mercenaries followed their Captain's order, popping off rounds while Ziler ran toward the boat.

He climbed onto the main deck. First, he knocked one of the fuel drums off the starboard side, submerging it in the lake. Next, he used the Bowie knife to pry the cap off the second fuel drum. Fresh gasoline spilled onto the side of the boat, drizzling into the river.

Ziler waited, giving the mosquitos enough time to crowd around him.

He yanked a flare stick from a cargo pocket in his pants, and broke the tip, sparking a large red flame.

Jumping off the boat, he chucked the flare onto the puddle of fuel. The gas ignited, the remaining contents in the drum rupturing in a huge, orange explosion.

Ziler could feel the heat on his back as he touched down, the force of the blast propelling him forward. Staying on his feet, he sprinted back for the hut, keeping his head low as Graves and Browne shot at a few eager mosquitos above his head.

He reentered the hut and watched the aftermath of his improvisation. Before long, the smoke filled the air, the deck of the ship completely ablaze. Just like at the facility, the mosquitos were driven off, the chemical composition in the air not agreeing with their respiratory systems.

"Looks like they're going," Graves said. "Nice work, Captain. Couldn't have done it better myself."

"That's probably the most polite thing I've ever heard you say," Ziler said. He took a breath, then looked over at Liz. She was crouched in the far corner of the hut, her throat tight, her eyes wide.

"So, what now?" she asked.

"At the moment?" Ziler said. "We wait. Hope you're not sensitive to smoke, because we're gonna let that thing burn for a while."

Graves began his ammo check. "Sounds perfectly fine with me."

Browne stepped forward, repeatedly pointing his thumb to the east.

Ziler knew the meaning: *What about Dr. Cabot and Wallington?*

"All we can do is hope they survived," he said. "Unfortunately, there's nothing we can do for them at the moment."

CHAPTER 13

When Susan Cabot was a young child, her father had taken her to Cedar Point repeatedly during summertime. He always thought she enjoyed riding the Monster, an octopus-shaped ride with spinning cars at the end of each arm. Her father thought she loved that ride, so he took her on it for what felt like a thousand times a day. She remembered one windy day, seated in one of the cars of that thing. Up and down, spinning around, wind in the face, all sense of direction lost, no sense of control—she just wanted the ride to end.

As she struggled in the water, Susan felt the exact same sensation…with the unwelcome addition of water entering her mouth. Up and down, side to side, she had lost all sense of direction. Every time she surfaced, the mosquitos were right there waiting for her. She had only a split-second to get a breath before submerging. There was no time to get her bearings. All she knew was she was in the deepest part of the river and was rapidly getting tired. She had no idea where Wallington was, or if he was even still alive.

She was never a great swimmer and could barely hold her breath for over a minute. The company had invested a lot of money in the research facility, including an extensive lounge area, but they never bothered to include fitness equipment. Her lack of exercise was evident in her pitiful attempt to swim. Her panicked mind did not help matters. As soon as she submerged, she was already feeling the need to fill her lungs with more air.

The buzzing of wings was still present. It was as though those horrible insects knew she would eventually surface. That, and they could probably see her under the water. She barely submerged below three feet. Even at that depth, the water took on a dark, murky quality. Not to mention, she could barely keep her eyes open when under.

Susan waited until she thought her lungs would burst, then went for the surface again. As before, two mosquitos were right there waiting for her. The doctor emerged and sucked in a partial breath, which was partially lost in a loud scream. She felt spindly legs touch her face and took in the reeking smell that radiated from their bodies.

Down she went, not even able to determine which direction the shore was. She tried swimming in one direction, hoping she would eventually reach shallower water. That course of action lasted twenty seconds before her body began protesting. Her muscles strained, as did her lungs. Next, her mind went into overdrive. In the middle of the chaos and fright came one horrible realization: Even if she made it to shore, the bugs would be right on top of her.

There was nowhere to go. Her only two choices were to drown or get fed upon. It was an impossible decision—she didn't want to die at all!

Pop! Pop! Pop! Pop!

Susan didn't know what she was listening to. These noises were muffled cracks of sound coming from somewhere above the water's surface.

Splash!

Susan turned around, her eyes now wide open in spite of her natural instinct. The mosquito was in the water with her.

Her scream came out with a flurry of air bubbles. Up for the surface she went. It was as though her body was fed up with the brain's indecisiveness and went on autopilot.

When she emerged, the sounds became much more distinct.

Bang-bang-bang! Bang-bang-bang!

Another bug hit the water.

Susan watched it crash down, then spun to her right. There on the south shore was Wallington. He was crouched on one knee, carefully picking off the remaining mosquitos that hovered over her.

Another flurry of bullets shredded the last mosquito. Its blood sprinkled into the river, preceding the *splash* of its limp body.

Wallington stood up and waved at Susan.

"Keep swimming, Doc. Over here."

With no giant bugs lingering over her head, Susan could finally concentrate. She completed a series of strokes, pulling herself closer to the shallow end of the river.

Her feet touched the bottom.

"Oh, thank God," she muttered. She walked the rest of the way, collapsing to her knees once she cleared the water's edge.

Wallington gave Susan a moment to catch her breath before pulling her to her feet. "We gotta go."

"Okay…" Another deep breath. "Thank you."

"No need to thank me, but we need to get moving," he said. "We need to… oh, crap."

A defeated look came over his face as he stared downriver. Susan turned around, seeing the cloud of smoke that alarmed him so much. It was hard to know for sure at this distance, but it appeared that the barge had gone ablaze.

"Is that them?" she said.

"Looks to be the case," he replied. He lifted a finger to his lips, requesting silence. Both of them listened, hearing the distant buzzing of wings coming from the plume of smoke.

"They're coming back," Susan said. "Where do we go?"

Wallington glanced around. There was no time to come up with a brilliant plan. All they could do was think on the fly and hope for the best. He faced the branch of water that led to the cove.

"This way. Maybe we can find a place to hunker down for a while."

They ran south, disappearing into the web of shadows cast by the low-hanging branches. Susan's wet clothes weighed her down, making each step an excruciating effort. The humidity didn't help matters either. Sweat mixed with grime and river water, making her feel like a slimy beast straight out of someone's demented imagination.

If I ever get out of here, I'm gonna move to a place where bugs wouldn't travel within a hundred miles of. Alaska, it is!

The unspoken joke was partially successful in alleviating the sense of terror she felt. The droning sound was several yards behind them now, probably near the mouth of the cove.

All of a sudden, Wallington stopped. He threw his hands out, signaling for her to halt.

Susan dug her feet into the ground, barely preventing herself from colliding with him.

"What is it?" A gasp quickly followed her question. The answer was right there in front of her.

They stood near the cove's main body, taking in the rank smell. It was a fleshy, rotten smell, similar, but different to that from the corpses. In this case, it was not the smell of death, but of new life. New, horrid life that God did not intend.

Floating in the cove were red, circular objects. Wallington and Susan both knew what they were looking at. Eggs. Hundreds of eggs, interconnected by a stringy, saliva substance. They were basketball-sized, their color red with the blood of hundreds of victims, human and animal. Their 'shell' was not rigid like chicken eggs, but were soft and somewhat translucent. Larval bodies wiggled within, awaiting their turn at life.

Susan put a hand over her mouth. They had stumbled right into the mosquitos' nest.

A pulsing motion from one of the eggs caught Susan's eye. It was twelve feet from shore, the shape inside wriggling like a fish on a line. The top of the egg split open. The basketball shape quickly deflated as the white, diaphanous shape emerged. It seemed to 'stand' on its rear end, slowly gaining its natural color. Six hair-thin legs extended from its segmented body.

The newest member of the mosquito swarm was born.

"Oh, Lord Almighty," Susan whispered.

Wallington looked over his shoulder toward the sound of approaching wings. He grabbed Susan by the shoulder and ran into the forest.

"Let's go!"

Into the trees they went. The vegetation was thick and blinding, the sun's rays fighting to get through.

"Where do we go?" she said.

"We'll find a place," Wallington said. "First, we need to put some distance between ourselves and—Whoa!"

Susan gasped, colliding into the mercenary who had unexpectedly stopped. His arms were outstretched, his feet dangling a few inches from the ground.

She stepped back, caught off guard by the sight of Wallington seemingly levitating. In the moments that followed, her brain registered the sight of the silky cloud that stretched between the trees. Its color was a mix between white and brown, the latter color likely coming from dirt and slime from the flora and insect life.

The mass, stretching for several yards between multiple trees, appeared like a cloud at first glance. The strands that made up its parts had been tightly weaved with intention. The cloud was still thin enough for her to see through it, aside from a few isolated portions.

Susan beheld the sight of tightly weaved, cylinder-shaped husks scattered throughout the cloud. Though different in size, each one was designed with a singular purpose: containment.

There were more of them on the ground, hollowed out, containing remnants of the prisoners they once held. Bird beaks. Reptile claws. Even the exoskeletons of mosquitos, white and void of flesh.

Reality struck, her suspicions confirmed when she saw the enormous funnel near the branch of a tree. She saw the long, brown legs protruding from its opening, their tips feeling the wiggling web strands.

Wallington had run into a gigantic spiderweb.

Like with the fish they claimed to have encountered, this spider probably managed to snag one of the experimental mosquitos while it was still relatively small. As a result, it had grown to monstrous proportions. The creature, whether intentionally or through sheer luck, had formed this giant web near the mosquito nest, essentially guaranteeing it a lifetime supply of food.

Today, it would get its first taste of human.

Susan felt the impulse to gag as the arachnid began to reveal itself. Its body was a mix between white and red, its eight eyes black as night, its pedipalps twitching. The legs expanded, tripling the width of its body.

"Jesus!" she croaked. She grabbed the medic and tried to pull him free. The sticky substance had a secure hold on him. He could feel the spider's approach through the vibration through the web.

The mercenary had been through a lot in his time, but there was no way he could be prepared for this fate. Death by bullets, explosions, chemical exposure, close combat—he was mentally ready for any of those potential fates.

Not being food for a giant spider.

Being an experienced medic, his training involved treating wounds from insect and arachnid bites. Thus, he knew how such creatures fed. Some species covered their prey in pre-digestive fluids, while others paralyzed them with venom and held them in a cocoon until it was time to drink their blood.

All sense of bravado was lost. Unable to muscle his way out of the web, he descended into sheer panic. His motions only served to quicken the spider's motions.

Susan pulled on his vest with all her might, but was unable to pull him free.

"Get out of here!" he shouted.

There was no time to argue. She backed away, only to trip and fall on her back. Susan sat up and looked at her foot, feeling her own panic attack setting in after seeing the strand of webbing that had snagged her foot. Her attempts to unsnag herself served only to nearly get her fingers caught in the sticky glaze that covered each strand.

It was as strong as it was sticky, refusing to break no matter how hard she tugged at it.

"Oh, God! Oh, God! Oh, God!" she muttered.

"Go!" Wallington shouted. He thrashed in place, his breathing intensifying, a scream suppressed within his lungs. He tried to reach for his pistol, pulling against the web in order to unclip the holster.

Time ran out. The arachnid was on top of him, its legs arching over his writhing body.

"GET AWAY FROM ME—AHHHH!"

Four long legs scooped him toward the pedipalps. For the briefest of moments, Susan saw the fangs protruding from their ends. The spider's body tensed as those fangs sank into the medic.

There was a quick yelp, then a slow groaning. Wallington's struggle came to a sudden stop, his body quickly tensing as the paralyzing venom surged through his veins.

The spider remained still, waiting for the process to complete. Wallington let out a groan. A white foamy substance accumulated in his mouth, dripping down his front. His entire body was stiff as a board. The spider leaned back and angled its abdomen under its head, its lower legs pulling new strands of web towards its catch. Its front legs managed to detach Wallington from the snag, then spun his body around, mummifying him in the silk cocoon.

Susan found herself equally paralyzed, not from venom, but fear. Once it was done cocooning Wallington, she would be next. She looked at the spot on the web where Wallington originally made contact. In his place was his rifle, a knife, and his radio, all dangling from web strands.

The thought of grabbing them came too late. Frolicking legs turned the spider in her direction.

Susan screamed. She got on her feet, ready to run. As she did, she noticed a black, circular shape near the right corner of the web. It was a hole. A *tunnel*. Probably left behind by an aardvark, in all likelihood. Regardless, it was big enough for her to hide in.

She crawled on all fours, then threw herself into the tunnel. It descended for two meters, widening as it went. To her relief, there was nothing inside waiting for her. Nothing but dirt.

The sound of scuffling near the entrance made her cringe. She looked back and squealed, seeing two long legs reaching into the pit.

Susan pressed herself against the back of the tunnel. She was encased in darkness, the only light coming from the tunnel's entrance, which was now obstructed by the arachnid's mass.

The legs, bending like caterpillars, closed within a few inches of her knees. They wiggled, desperately searching for her.

In one brisk motion, they retracted.

Susan opened her eyes, seeing the little bit of sunlight at the tunnel's entrance. The spider had moved away, its legs ruffling the undergrowth around the tunnel.

She could hear mosquito wings nearby. The spider had probably gone to either repel an intruder or catch it for food. Either way, it seemed to have forgotten about her.

Minutes went by, during which Susan did not move a muscle. Every breath was shallow. There was a fear that the slightest sound, even from breathing, would attract the spider.

The web near the entrance wiggled intensely as a heavy mass scaled its height. She leaned forward for a better view, catching a glimpse of one of its rear legs. It was returning to its funnel-shaped hideout.

Her sense of relief only came with a new wave of terror. She was trapped in this tunnel without food or water. Her foot was still caught by an outstretched strand of web. The only way out would put her in the path of that spider. Even if she got away, she would only end up near the mosquito nest.

It was a similar predicament as when she was in the river, but worse. There, her options were either drown or be killed by mosquitos. Now, it was either get eaten by a spider, have her blood sucked by mosquitos, or starve to death in a dark, damp tunnel.

Being a doctor, she knew better than most that starvation was no joke. It was a slow, horrible way to die. She wished she remained in the river. Drowning was a horrible fate, but she would rather suffer that than this. Yet, she couldn't bring herself to step outside. The only thing worse than starvation was the fate of being imprisoned in a spiderweb, waiting to endure the horrible fate of being fed upon.

She buried her face in her hands.

This can't be happening!

CHAPTER 14

"Wallington? If you can hear me, acknowledge this transmission."

Ziler groaned. He knew that if Wallington was alive, he would already know to radio the others. It was standard procedure, and frankly, common sense in situations like these. The only exceptions were if he was near an enemy position and needed to remain absolutely quiet.

Ziler took a seat and watched the small bonfire crackle outside the hut's entrance. The boat fire had been extinguished, the deckhouse scavenged for any supplies they could use. There wasn't much; just some canned food, water bottles, a fire axe, a flare pistol, and things to burn. That's all the boat was good for at this point—burning. They tore off whatever scraps they could and lit three fires around the hut, forming a sort of blockade against any bugs that happened to fly in this direction. Graves and Browne were both outside, scavenging for other supplies while the coast was clear.

"Still nothing?" Liz said.

A hundred different replies ran through Ziler's mind. It was probably the most pathetic attempt to sound concerned he'd ever heard. It was amazing, after all of her antics leading up to this point, that Liz Moore honestly thought she came off as compassionate.

Then again, considering her drug-baked mind...

He shook his head.

"That's a real shame," Liz said, exhaling sharply, unconvincingly feigning remorse.

"Yeah, a real shame," Ziler said. "Descher, Medford, Morales, Ankrum—all a damn shame."

Her brow furrowed. "You blame me?"

"You're goddamn right I do."

Liz uncrossed her arms, her jaw dropping as though she was astonished he would feel this way. It came as no surprise Dr. Liz Moore was the type who was not challenged often, if ever.

"You're a man of war," she said. "I would've thought you of all people should've known what he was getting his team into."

"That's the problem," Ziler said. "I *didn't* know what I was getting myself into. You were deliberately vague, implying it may have been warlords or bandits. Not genetically engineered animal life."

Liz shook her head. "I didn't know…"

"You did know," Ziler said. "Or, at least, suspected. You were so focused on keeping your little secret, you forgone all common sense."

"We can compensate you for the lost men," Liz said.

There it was. This was the reason Dr. Liz Moore was put in control of this operation. The company needed someone who saw people as numbers on a checklist. A cost on a budget. Pieces on a chessboard. She assumed that Ziler, being a mercenary, had no value on human life.

He chose not to respond to that. Doing so would only initiate a back-and-fourth with her. Already, he was tempted to throw her sorry ass in the river and leave her behind. If anyone on this trip deserved it, it was Liz.

Liz, oblivious as she was, took his silence as an agreement to her proposal. Thinking the matter was settled, she stood up.

"Well, the chopper's not gonna hang around forever," she said. "When do we leave?"

"I'm gonna give Wallington a little more time."

"It's already been an hour," Liz said.

"I'm not writing him off. Or Susan, for that matter," he said.

"I think we need to face the fact that they've been killed," Liz said. "They fell overboard. There were mosquitoes everywhere. It's unlikely—"

Ziler stood up. "I'll tell you what facts to face." Liz leaned against the wall, caught off guard by his imposing voice. Ziler towered over her, looking as though he was staring at a pile of garbage. "We're giving them more time. If we need to, we'll go back and look for them."

"Even if that gets the rest of us killed?" Liz said.

"If you were so concerned about safety, you wouldn't have been running this experiment in the first place."

She shook her head. "You don't understand."

"I don't understand?" Ziler snickered. "I understand plenty. Quite frankly, I understand better than you do."

"If we didn't come up with this…"

"Yeah, yeah, yeah. 'If we didn't come up with this, someone else would have'," Ziler said. "Like I said, I understand better than you do."

He went outside. At this point, he would rather fight another swarm of mosquitos than sit in the hut listening to Liz try and justify the company's experimentations.

Browne was standing guard, watching the sky above the river. Sooner or later, the bugs would return.

The time was around sixteen-hundred hours. Six hours until sunset. If the bugs functioned like their normal-sized counterparts, they would be twice as active at night.

Ziler knew he needed to make a decision. Either make a desperate attempt to reach the rendezvous point or go back and find Wallington and Susan.

The method of travel had already been determined. Graves proudly marched up the shoreline, dragging an abandoned dugout canoe. It was twelve feet in length and contained two wooden oars.

"A motorboat would be more useful, but then again, I guess beggars can't be choosers," Graves said.

"Any more of these?" Ziler asked.

"Two others."

"Good." Ziler inspected the sides of the canoe. "We can build torches and have them stand tall. That might help keep the bugs off our asses."

"We'll put that other fuel drum to use," Graves said. "I saw you knock that thing into the water before you torched the boat. I know what you were thinking. Could put that fuel to use."

"I guess you're not as dumb as you look," Ziler said.

Graves cocked his head back, unsure whether to take that as an insult or a compliment.

"We taking the lady along?" he said, tilting his head toward the hut.

Ziler sighed. "Yeeeaaah."

Graves shared the same unspoken opinion. He would gladly leave the bitch here to rot. Sometimes, he hated being the good guy.

"Still no word from Wallington?"

Ziler shook his head. "I'm gonna try again in a minute. Just needed to get away from the doc."

"Can't blame you there," Graves said. He looked east down the river. "Don't know about you, Cap, but I'm starting to think about retirement."

"Is that right?" Ziler said. He was partly amused. Graves was always eager for the next mission. The thrill of the gig was better than the money. "It's hard to imagine you living the quiet life."

"Yeah, but it's harder to imagine fighting alongside everyone else," Graves said. He looked quietly at the river. There was a heavy concentration in his eyes, as though he saw *through* the river and the rainforest, at the ghosts of his brothers who recently perished. "Most of our guys are dead. Over sixty missions, and hardly a scratch among us. Next thing we know, we're here, and everything's changed. I figure this mission is the ultimate test of our strength. God's way of saying we've done enough."

Ziler stood beside him and watched the water. Sixty missions, and never once did he ever hear the obnoxious, foul-mouthed Graves say anything even close to poignant.

"Yeah. Maybe you're right," he said.

"You thinking of bringing down the company?" Graves whispered.

Ziler nodded. "This situation can't be swept under the rug. It may sound extreme, but this stupid company is playing with fire. You heard what Susan Cabot said about these bugs, how fast they propagate."

"So, basically, we're saving the world," Graves said. He put his fists on his hips, puffed his chest out, and grinned proudly. The only thing missing was a cape blowing in the wind and some triumphant music playing in the background. "Yeah, when we put it that way, I guess it's fitting to have this as the last mission. Can't really top saving the world."

Ziler smirked. "I suppose you can't." He tapped Graves on the shoulder. "Grab one of the other canoes. I'm gonna try radioing Wallington again."

"You got it, boss."

CHAPTER 15

After thirty minutes in the burrow, Susan's muscles started to cramp. After an hour, she felt pins and needles in her left foot. Even with the annoying sensation, she refused to budge. Any kind of motion might attract the horrible fiend outside.

Another hour went by. Her clothes, still wet from the river, were now caked with dirt. She had been sweating nonstop since arriving ashore, sparking intense thirst. Her mouth was dry, her stomach cramping, her skin itching due to the ants and other tiny insects that lurked in this tunnel.

She was coated in darkness, the little light several feet ahead gradually starting to fade.

Eventually, two hours turned to three.

In that course of time, she had heard calls from Captain Ziler. He had survived and was making a desperate attempt to get in contact with Wallington, unaware of his fate.

Every so often, she could hear him moan. He was still alive in that cocoon. She had hoped that the venom had killed him. Instead, it prolonged his suffering. Not only was he alive, he was conscious, completely aware of the horrors that awaited him. He also probably heard Ziler's radio transmissions, which triggered an unquiet desperation to escape from this predicament.

After a while, the transmissions stopped.

Susan could not suppress the tears. She wanted to get to that radio and call for help, but going out there would only mean her doom. Her way out of this mess was so close, yet so far.

"God, why?" she whispered. "I didn't know what I was in for. I thought I was doing the right thing. I'm sorry for being involved with this company. I'm sorry for all of those I have hurt. I didn't mean to hurt all of those people. I'm sorry. I guess… maybe I deserve this." She looked up, not at the layer of sediment, but at the heavens far above. "If I could, I would trade places with Wallington. He's a good person. Better than me. He deserves to be here less than I do. He's actually saved lives." A sigh followed the statement. "I just wish I could save at least *one* person before I leave this world."

Susan lowered her head. She had heard someone say something about never losing faith, no matter how tough things got. Though she was never good at practicing religion, that lesson always stuck.

It seemed impossible, even for God to get her out of this scenario. She was in a small underground tunnel with a giant spider outside. Even if she peeked, it would be right on her, ready to wrap her in a cocoon and stash her next to Wallington.

It's too easy to remain defeated. You HAVE to rise above the difficulty, no matter what it is.

That internal lecture was all she could do to not lose faith.

Out of nowhere, hope arrived. After the events of the last couple of days, Susan would never have been optimistic to hear the sounds of mosquito wings. At least one of the bugs was wandering near the web, probably in search of fresh blood.

She leaned forward to peek out of the tunnel entrance. The web was still at first. All of a sudden, it started to wiggle.

The fluttering of wings took on a similar, but different sound. They were only partially flapping, their whirring now taking on a higher pitch like a buzzsaw cutting through wood.

She watched as the web fluttered with increased intensity. The mosquito was snagged.

The web shifted as a tremendous weight moved on the upper corner on the opposite side. She felt the urge to vomit, knowing that the spider was making its way toward the mosquito.

Fear nearly paralyzed Susan. *Nearly*.

She thought of Wallington.

"If I can save at least one person before I leave this world…"

She expelled her fear in a high-pitched whine as she shifted her weight. Slowly, Susan made her way up the burrow. Two feet from the entrance, she could look up out of the web.

Indeed, the spider had emerged, its legs sprawled out. Two yards in front of it was the unlucky mosquito, flailing right next to Wallington's cocoon. It had probably spotted him and saw an opportunity for an easy meal. Now, it was seconds away from joining him.

The spider moved in, slowly at first, then with a surprising burst of speed. The whirring of wings came to a sudden stop.

Susan yelped, barely suppressing a scream. The spider sank its fangs into the mosquito, dripping venom into its body.

Hanging a few feet from the ground was Wallington's radio.

The arachnid's attention was firm on the bug, with no awareness for the rest of the world in these precious moments.

Susan counted down from three, took a shaky breath, then sprang from the tunnel. Her cramped muscles fought against her, making her movements clumsy and awkward. Rather than run to the radio, she made a fast hobble towards it.

The spider was pulling the mosquito up the length of the web and was beginning the cocooning process. Susan had a minute at most.

She grabbed the radio and pulled. Go figure, the stupid device was snagged tightly. Though there were only a few strands that clung to it, they were strong as steel.

"Come on!"

She pulled harder, stretching the web, but not breaking it.

The nest shifted. Susan looked up.

The spider had ceased cocooning the mosquito, its many eyes now fixed on her.

"Oh, no..." She tugged again. "Get off!"

The spider started making its way toward its new meal, crawling over Wallington.

Susan hyperventilated. She was free and clear of the strand that held her. She could just run and take her chances.

Yet, she could not forget her promise to not leave Wallington behind.

She looked at the radio. Dangling next to it was Wallington's pistol, caught firmly in the web.

She grabbed ahold of it, redirected the muzzle at the spider, then pulled the trigger.

Bang!

Susan jumped, unconditioned for the recoil and deafening blast. Her aim, however, was spot on. The spider scurried backward, its front legs and mandibles frolicking over its face. It had taken a hit.

Susan pulled the radio as far as she could, then put the muzzle to the web strands.

Bang! Bang! Bang!

The bullets cut through the strong silk, freeing the radio.

Her ringing ears picked up the sound of intense droning coming from the cove. The gunshots had probably rattled the swarm of mosquitos. Running was no option. She had no choice but to duck back into the burrow.

Her muscles now loose, she sprinted for the tunnel and slipped inside, keeping the radio close to her body. The spider made its way down the web and clawed at the entrance.

Just like before, it quickly got distracted by the arrival of mosquitos. It raced back up to the nest, ready to defend its cocoons and maybe catch additional prey.

Susan rested on her elbows and inspected the radio. She found the transmitter and pressed it. A tiny green light near the antennae lit up.

"H-hello? Is anyone out there? Captain Ziler? Anyone? Please respond."

***

Ziler perked up. A voice came through his hand-held unit. Browne and Graves turned to face him, their faces mirroring the same awe he was experiencing. For the last several hours, Ziler had tried unsuccessfully to gain contact. Up until five seconds ago, he was ready to assume the worst.

"This is Ziler. Is that you, Dr. Cabot?"

"Oh, thank God. Yes. Yes, it's me."

"Where are you? Are you hurt? Where's Wallington?"

"I'm okay for now, but I can't move. I'm hiding in a burrow near a large—prep yourselves for this one—spiderweb."

Graves hung his head back and let out a pitiful groan. "Oh, fantastic. I hate spiders!"

122

"Wallington's in the web. He's paralyzed, but still alive."

"Jesus." Ziler looked away, taking a moment to comprehend the situation. Even now, it was hard to fathom a real-life giant spider.

"Captain, there's something else."

By the sound of her voice, he knew whatever she was about to say was of grave importance.

"I'm listening."

"Remember that cove we passed during the attack? The one you told me not to go down?"

"I do."

"At its end is a nest. A huge, freaking nest. Its full of mosquito eggs."

Graves and Browne instinctively clutched their weapons. Ziler looked at them and nodded. Already, they knew what had to be done.

"How many bugs are in the area?"

"I've been hearing a lot of movement lately. The temperature's starting to drop a little. They're probably all over the place right now."

"Copy that. Stand by, Doctor." Ziler turned his attention to his men. "Three of us, a hundred or so of them."

Browne snorted. *My kind of odds.*

"What the gimp here is trying to say…" Graves tilted his head at Browne, who gave him a bitter glance, "…is we might have an opportunity to stop this outbreak in its tracks. These bugs have only been multiplying for two weeks. Considering the number of eggs in that nest, it's probable they haven't set up camp elsewhere as of yet."

"Are you guys crazy?" Liz said.

"Crazy? For trying to clean up your mess?" Graves said. "No. You're the crazy one, Doc. Go back in the hut and snort. Hell, take in the whole ball all at once. Think of it as a personal challenge."

"Fuck you," Liz said. She looked to Ziler as though he might be a voice of reason. "Captain, going back there is a suicide run. Look." She pointed at the canoes. "We have a way out of here. You've got the torches burning. The bugs are concentrated behind us. We might be able to get out of this. Once we get back, we can get a properly equipped crew out here."

"I'm sure you're already working on your cover story," Ziler said.

"Yeah," Graves said, chuckling. "'Breaking: Rival company... insert name here... has been conducting experiments in Congo Rainforest, resulting in an outbreak of giant mosquitos that threaten the world.'"

Liz faced Ziler, her face red. "Does he ever shut up?"

Ziler cracked a grin. "Dr. Moore, you've achieved something more spectacular, so monumental, that it's worthy of the Nobel Peace Prize... you've made me appreciate the sound of Grave's voice. When compared to yours, it's like listening to the birds sing in springtime."

Graves gave a big smile. "Why, thank you, Captain."

"*Only* when compared to her insistent clucking," Ziler said. "Trust me, once we get on a flight out of here, I'm sure I'm gonna wish the mosquitos got your ass."

Graves shrugged. "I'll take whatever praise I can get."

Ziler shook his head. "Susan, you still there?"

"I'm here."

"Hang tight. We're coming to get you."

"And just how the hell you plan on doing that?" Liz said. "This is suicide. There's no gain from going back. I'm sorry, Captain, but your man's dead. There's no value in Dr. Cabot. If we go back, we'll get killed. But if we leave now, we might be able to make it back around nightfall. Don't know about you, but I'm not eager to spend the night out in this jungle."

"Dr. Moore. Always a displeasure to hear your voice," Susan said.

"At least I'm not foolish enough to wander near a giant spiderweb," Liz said. "Sorry, Dr. Cabot. We can't help you. Maybe if you can hold on until the rescue team arrives..." Liz failed to hide her sinister smile.

"Hey, bitch? Might wanna check your vest pocket."

Liz's smile vanished. Slowly, her hand felt her vest. Her eyes widened. Frantically, she searched all her pockets. The thumb drive and the two samples were missing.

"Oh, no. Oh, no."

"Captain, is she freaking out?"

"To put it mildly," Ziler replied, watching Liz with mild amusement.

Liz turned to face him, then lunged for the radio. "Where the hell is it?! How'd you get it?!"

"Well, if you weren't so fixated on your 'habit', you would've noticed me lifting them off you. Now, they're in my pocket. Believe me, I'll make sure the last thing I do before I die is smash your samples and your precious thumb drive. Considering the damage the explosion has done to the lab's computers, you'd have to start from scratch. Enjoy explaining that one to the board of directors."

"Dr. Cabot, I swear—"

Ziler pushed her away. "That's enough, Dr. Moore. Susan, what's your position in relation to the cove?"

"Maybe a hundred yards southwest."

"Understood. Stay put. Give us time. We'll figure something out."

"Thank you."

Ziler turned to his men. "Well, boys, it looks like we have one more big fight before retirement."

Graves smiled. "Damn right. I'm ready for one last fight. I mean, it sounds kinda ridiculous when you realize it's giant mosquito monsters we're saving the world from, but all the same, let's kick ass." He held his fist to Ziler. The Captain rolled his eyes, then went along with the gesture, bumping fists with both Graves and Browne. "I'm assuming you already have a plan."

Ziler looked to Browne. "How many explosives do we have?"

Browne raised four fingers.

Right there, Graves' question was answered. "Blow up the nest... best plan ever."

"Four blocks of C4. Might need more than that to destroy that nest," Ziler said.

"The nice doctor said the place is crawling with mosquitos," Graves said, gladly taking notice of the shift in Liz's expression. "Fighting them off is gonna be tricky. We're good shots, but there's probably more bugs than we have bullets. Unless we find a giant can of mosquito spray out here, we're gonna have a hard time even getting near that place."

Ziler thought for a moment. Those two words 'can' and 'spray' triggered a wild, but possible alternative. He glanced at the spare fuel drum in the canoe and the burning torches towering from the two ends.

"What's on your mind?" Graves said.

"Dig through the boat," Ziler said. "Look for any rubber hoses. We're gonna make a quick stop before paying a visit to Mosquito-Daycare."

CHAPTER 16

The trip down the river was silent and hot. The torches burned furiously, masking the mercenaries' scent and deterring any insects from investigating. Every stroke of the oars was smooth and gentle, their handlers careful not to make any noise that would alert the swarm.

A quarter-mile past the cove, they arrived at the abandoned camp. A relic of a war that ended over a century ago, it had remained untouched, despite all of the expeditions, rebellions, and expansion the Congo had endured.

They brought the two canoes ashore, the second one containing the fuel drum. Immediately, they began ransacking the camp. Old provisions, weapons, and ammo were stored in steel crates. Those that were left outside were rusted and damp. Those that were kept inside the containers were in surprisingly decent condition, though not useful for the team's purposes.

Liz stood by the canoe, her arms crossed like a disgruntled teenager who was grounded by her parents. She watched bitterly, not bothering to lend a helping hand while the team scavenged the old camp.

Graves was in the broken-down fort, opening a metal crate with a rusted prybar. The lid had rusted shut, making the effort to open it a tedious one. He bit his lip, cursing under his breath as he fought against the thing.

"The hell did they keep in here?" Finally, the rust gave way and the lid popped open. Graves peeked inside. That never-ending smirk on his face vanished. "Whoa!"

Browne ran over to him, looked inside the crate, then pulled his brother-in-arms away from it.

"What's the matter?" Ziler said. He hopped off the boat and ran over to them.

"Oh, nothing," Graves said. "Just nearly blew my ass into a bunch of tiny bits."

Ziler glanced into the crate. Inside were over a hundred sticks of dynamite. Each one was sweating nitroglycerin. Now it was clear what Graves meant, for these explosives, after being kept in hundred-degree heat for a century, were highly unstable.

"Okay. Open every crate with extreme caution from here on," Ziler said.

"Was this what you were looking for?" Graves said.

"No, but we might be able to put this to use," Ziler said. "We'll load this onto the second canoe and float it into the cove. We'll set the charges and eradicate that nest."

"That's fabulous," Graves said. "But that still leaves the question of 'how are we gonna get near it?' I doubt we can just push the canoe into the cove and hope for the best. It'll drift left or right before it gets anywhere near the nest."

Ziler responded with a confident smile. He gestured for the two men to follow him to the boat.

They stepped aboard the rusty hunk of metal, the stale smell filling their noses. Ziler led them through the lower decks, shining a flashlight to guide the way. The interior of the boat was sealed tight, protected by multiple layers of thick steel. With the lights not functional, it was like walking through the catacombs of an old abandoned building.

They arrived in the cargo hold. Dozens of rifles and pistols were stored on racks. Though not as badly as the weapons outside, they were rusted, their components stiff from being left unattended for so long.

"Gosh, we could make a killing if we sold all of this shit to a museum," Graves said. "Not sure if it's gonna help us kill the bugs though."

Ziler directed him to a large, steep crate. "No, but this might."

Graves approached the object. It was larger than the other crates and rectangular in shape. It had been sealed tight for over a century, up until five minutes ago when Ziler first inspected it. Graves opened it.

"Oh, now this is cool." Inside was a large cylinder-shaped container, with a piece of hose connecting it to a long metal rod.

"An M.1916 Kleif Flammenwerfer, used by the Germans in World War One," Ziler said.

"You can just call it a flamethrower," Graves said. He lifted the old weapon from its crate. Its components, though requiring a little tuning, were in remarkably good condition considering their age. Under normal circumstances, this weapon would not be his first option. However, he was confident he would be able to make it work for limited use.

Browne took the nozzle and handed the tank to Graves. *I'll operate the nozzle, you wear the harness.*

"Hey!" Graves protested. "Who said you get to torch the bugs with this?"

Browne responded with a middle finger.

"I say he wins the argument," Ziler said.

"Figures," Graves said. "You never side with me."

"Exactly. Besides, I know Browne knows how to handle this thing."

"Yeah? How'd you know that?" Graves said.

"Because he reads. Obviously, you don't realize this thing requires two men to operate."

"Oh, ha-ha." Graves inspected the rod and the hose. The hose was spongy, having deteriorated over time. He smiled. Now it made sense why Ziler wanted them to take any hoses from the barge.

"You think you can do a makeshift job with the spray hose we took off the barge?" Ziler asked him.

"It won't look pretty," Graves said. "There'll be a lot of electrical tape involved, but I can make it work."

"Get to it then," Ziler said. "We're running out of daylight, and Susan and Wallington are running out of time."

CHAPTER 17

What's taking them so long?

Susan was trying her best not to be impatient. She was fully aware of what the mercenaries were up against. Plus, she had seen the fire from the smoking barge. They probably had to make their way to the cove on foot. If they were able to travel by river, they weren't doing it with a motor. For all she knew, they had been ambushed by mosquitos again and killed.

She refused to entertain that thought. Following her 'keep the faith' discipline, she chose to believe Ziler's team was alive and well, strategically planning their attack.

For now, all she could do was stay alive. It was later in the evening now. Probably six. It was getting darker outside, the sun's rays heavily obscured by the rainforest. She could still see the web through the tunnel. So far, there was no movement since she spoke with Ziler over the radio.

Every so often, Wallington would groan. It was a mix of panic and pain. For Susan, it was simultaneously haunting and alleviating. As horrible as his situation was, at least he was still alive. If the team managed to get here in time, they would be able to cut him down and grant her the opportunity to save his life.

The fact that he was still alive after all these hours indicated that the venom wasn't fatal. There was still the risk of bacterial infection that made its way into the bite wounds. If the spider didn't kill him, the bacteria would after a day or two. The paralysis itself would probably begin to wear off after twenty-four hours, sooner if he received the proper medical treatment.

The facility in the village should have what he needs. I just need to get him there.

She felt a ping of hope.

It vanished after a moment, with a tidal wave of fear taking its place.

The web shook. It was gentle at first, a subtle shift generated by slow movements. Wallington was starting to groan more intensely now.

The spider was emerging. Perhaps it was the dimmed sunlight or the somewhat cooler temperatures of the early evening. Regardless of the outside factors, one thing was clear: it was feeding time.

Part of Susan wanted to shut her eyes and cover her ears. The other part of her needed to look at it. It wasn't curiosity or a fascination to watch it feed—she felt neither—but she needed to gauge its position from Wallington.

She moved to the entrance and peered up at the web, cringing when she saw the spider's outstretched legs. It was moving towards a cocoon that was placed a few feet beside Wallington. The mosquito that was held captive there started to shift, as if it knew that its ticket was about to be punched.

Wallington was able to move his head slightly. He was gritting his teeth, dripping a foamy saliva substance. He had regained enough muscular control to form words. Two words in particular.

"F-fuck you."

The spider took no notice of the insult, instead going straight for its appetizer. It towered over the paralyzed mosquito and extended its jaws. Dark fangs, attached to soft pedipalps, dangled over the mosquito before penetrating its shell.

After a few short moments, the spider retracted its fangs.

Susan watched in both awe and disgust. In that moment, she realized how this spider fed. She was no arachnologist, but she knew that spiders did not drink blood, but broke their prey down with digestive juices. Usually, that happened immediately upon the injection of venom. This spider, however, did not inject its enzymes until a few minutes prior to feeding.

"Must be a side effect of the mutation. Maybe the enzymes break down its prey faster than the usual arachnid," Susan said to herself. She noticed how the mosquito had stopped shuddering within its cocoon. The venom kept it paralyzed, but allowed it to stay alive so its meat would be fresh for feeding time. Now, its cellular structure was breaking down.

Two minutes passed. The spider extended its pink, fleshy feeding apparatus into the mosquito's cocoon.

Susan felt herself grow pale. She would never look at smoothies the same way again.

The spider fed at its leisure, its next victim shivering in his confinement. He knew he was next.

"Oh, Jesus," Susan muttered. The very thought of a human being undergoing what that bug went through was nauseating. "Come on, Ziler. Hurry up, please."
***

They huddled near their precious eggs, the larvae within gladly feeding on the blood their parents had provided. There was no affection for their elders, nor was there appreciation for their efforts. It was simply a matter of function.

The mosquitos existed to hunt and reproduce. Killing was as instinctual as breathing. Simple organisms, their minds unclouded by doubt, morality, or empathy. The only awareness of life and death was of their own. They only saw their victims as sources of blood. Nothing more or less.

The bugs were unaware of their dwindling numbers. Already, the swarm had forgotten the ferocious encounters with the human team that claimed many of its members. Remorse did not exist. They felt no anxiety or awareness of the future. All that mattered were the two primary goals—to feed and reproduce.

Their simultaneous slumber came to an end. Having wiped out much of the animal life in these many acres of forest, the amount of carbon dioxide in the air had fallen drastically. All at once, the swarm detected new traces of carbon dioxide being emitted near the cove's entrance.

Swallowing the delicious odor, they turned north. Many of them took to the air, ready to slurp the delicious blood from the foolish organisms that wandered near their hideout.

"Hear that?" Ziler said.

Browne nodded. He raised the nozzle of his flamethrower toward the droning sound up ahead. Graves was right behind him, rifle in hand. The tank, recently filled with gasoline from the fuel drum, was on his back. A few feet behind him was Liz Moore.

"Is it too much for me to ask for my gun back?" she whispered. "I mean, shit, we're heading directly into their nest."

Ziler gave it a moment's thought. Though he wasn't fully comfortable with arming her, the doctor did have a point. He pulled her pistol from his vest and tossed it over to her.

"Do anything stupid, and I'll feed you to those mosquitos myself."

Liz smirked, loading a fresh magazine into the gun. She did not offer a retort. Not that she needed to. Her thoughts were practically being broadcast at high frequency.

Ziler focused on the task at hand. They worked their way up the stream, leaving their canoes ashore. The task of loading the dynamite case into the spare canoe was a slow and tedious one. There was no margin for error, as the slightest bump could set the thing off.

As they gained distance, the droning sound up ahead intensified. In the blink of an eye, the bugs appeared. Dozens of them arrived at once, dropping altitude with intent to attack.

The team stopped in their tracks and took firing positions. Ziler fired multiple bursts, dropping two hostiles.

"Now's the time, Browne."

The silent mercenary pointed the mouth of the steel python at the gathering. Like a mythical dragon of ancient times, the machine fulfilled its purpose. A river of red-hot flames spat from the nozzle and surged into the swarm.

In the blink of an eye, the sky above flickered with dancing flames attached to multiple flying bodies. Mosquitos, their nerves screaming from the sudden heat, zipped in all directions, having forgotten about the meal below. Within seconds, they started dropping, their thin wings quickly burned away.

Browne kept up the punishment, steering the constant stream of fire as though flying a kite.

The bugs twirled in the air, attempting to dodge the flames while simultaneously closing in on the humans below.

Ziler put another bug in his crosshairs, shredding its thorax with three well-placed bullets. He adjusted his aim, setting his sights on another mosquito. It was coming right at him, avoiding the string of fire. Ziler squeezed the trigger.

Bang-bang-bang-bang!

The wings stopped flapping, its body dropping to the ground. Ziler confirmed his kill, then continued picking off stragglers while Browne continued paving the way.

The team inched closer to the cove. Gradually, the number of insects began to dwindle. Flying bodies of fire zipped in the clearing between the trees, like angels who had descended into hell. Those bodies quickly hit the ground, their boiling insides bursting through pores in their shell.

Liz even joined in the action, successfully planting several rounds into a mosquito that attempted to circle around them.

"Having fun there, buddy?" Graves said to Browne. The merc answered by directing his flame at a trio of mosquitos hovering over the stream. Their attempt to evade failed, the fire grabbing ahold of their bodies and brutally eating them away.

Like falling meteors, dead bugs encased in flame rained down in all directions.

After a few moments, there were less than a dozen insects in the area. Those that were not hit by the fire were kept at bay by its heat, making them easy targets for the riflemen.

Graves joined in the action, gleefully putting several bullets into one of the bugs.

"Can't wait to talk to my neighborhood exterminator…" Graves said. "He likes to brag about all the pests he has to deal with. Ha! He's gonna have a heart attack when he hears this story."

"No shit," Ziler said. He reloaded his M27, immediately planting a few rounds into another bug. Its abdomen split open, its insides raining down. Even with nothing to contain the blood it would intake, the injured mosquito still tried to lunge at him. Another shot struck it right in the mouth. The bony proboscis twirled like a baton in midair, landing somewhere in the grass. Its owner spiraled to the ground, its wings still flapping.

Browne hit a duo of bugs, roasting them.

Another minute of combat followed, during which the remaining hostiles were eliminated.

Browne sealed the nozzle, ceasing the stream of flame. The mercenaries looked every which way. The only mosquitos in the area were lying on the ground, dead and burning.

Graves stood up, smiling victoriously. "I think we got 'em."

"I don't see any more," Liz said.

"I'll break out the champagne when we blow this nest," Ziler said. He led the others down the shoreline. As they neared the destination, the stench of egg sacks and blood strengthened, overpowering even that of multiple burning corpses.

They arrived at the cove and laid eyes on the grotesque nest. Basketball-sized eggs, each containing developing larvae, floated in the shallow water. They were interconnected by some kind of membrane, like mucus in color and texture. Coagulated blood from hundreds of different animals draped the nest.

"Jesus," Liz said.

"There's hundreds," Graves said. "Thousands, maybe."

Ziler watched as one of the eggs twitched violently. The thin casing split open at the top, the sides shrinking in as a pale shape emerged through its top. He didn't wait long enough to see the legs and wings expand for the first time. With a squeeze of the trigger, the mosquito's life ended as quickly as it began.

"Won't be long before the others hatch," Graves said. He glanced at the forest. "Where'd the doc say she was hiding again?"

Ziler turned his attention to the forest. Dr. Cabot had stated her position was roughly a hundred yards southwest of the cove.

"Captain? You there?!"

"Oh, speak of the devil," Graves said.

"We're at the cove right now," Ziler said into his radio.

"Please hurry!"

"Yell out. Help me find you," Ziler said.

An ear-piercing scream echoed through the forest. Ziler pinpointed its source and led his team into the forest.

Susan's estimation of a hundred yards was almost right on the money. Ziler weaved past trees and undergrowth, slowing as he spotted the big white haze in the distance.

He came to a stop as his brain registered the sight of the eight-legged monstrosity standing on the web.

Graves and Browne stopped beside him, the former swallowing in an attempt to resist the urge to regurgitate.

"Holy…"

Even Browne looked unnerved, his busted jaw managing to mutter a single, stifled exclamation. "Fuck."

In this unique instance, Ziler was hesitant to engage. Rarely did fear get the better of him. Even giant insects and fish failed to rattle his nerves. Yet, nothing on planet Earth could prepare him for the sight of a gigantic-freaking-spider twitching on the side of its web, draining the remains of one of its victims. He could see every revolting detail of its body, every bulge in its exoskeleton, the texture in its eyes, and could hear the slurping sound… which disgustingly sounded like the last droplets of a milkshake being drained through a plastic straw.

It was lifting its head from the now-hollow cocoon, its fleshy tentacle-like mouthpiece dangling between its pedipalps. The arachnid seemed to take no notice of the mercenaries as it moved toward the next cocoon.

Ziler recognized the next victim right away. Wallington was still alive, groaning and wriggling in his restraints. His eyes were nearly bulging from their sockets, his teeth clenched tight, his mind surging with terror.

Nothing, not even the fear of an impossibly large spider, was going to stop Ziler from letting his medic become chowder. Pointing the M27 high, he fired several rounds.

The spider jolted, feeling the numerous impacts against its exoskeleton. More gunshots struck, one of which penetrated its left pedipalp. The spider scurried back from Wallington at a remarkable speed, confused as to what was happening. It turned in place in search of an intruder. Finally, it tilted its head upward to aim its eight eyes at Ziler.

His next several shots landed, but failed to kill the thing. Unlike the mosquitos, this spider was able to take a licking and keep on ticking. It scurried down the web, making contact with the earth. Standing upright, it looked larger than ever.

Ziler backed up and loaded a fresh magazine.

"Where's a giant boot when you need one?" Graves said.

The spider darted in their direction, hissing angrily.

The three mercenaries put their weapons on full-auto and unloaded into the beast. An onslaught of bullets cut into the spider's face, exploding its eight eyes. Yet, even after all the abuse, it kept coming.

Blind, but still alive, it sprang at them, its legs thumping the earth.

The mercenaries evaded in separate directions.

Ziler dove to his left, summersaulting to his feet. The spider continued racing, blindly colliding with a tree. Rolling onto its side, it flailed its legs ferociously, each limb seeking out its human foe.

Ziler pulled a grenade from his vest, pulled the pin, and made a softball-style toss toward the big arachnid. The resulting *boom* separated the spider's head from its abdomen and severed many of its legs. Jointed limbs hit the ground, twitching like unearthed worms. The remaining legs coiled under the abdomen, which spilled green guts onto the forest floor.

"Oh, thank God."

Ziler turned to the sound of Susan's voice. She crawled from the burrow, her clothes dirty and damp.

"Don't I get any credit?" he said.

The exhausted Susan gave a weak smile. "I suppose so. Thank you, Captain. You guys seem to be making a habit out of saving my life."

Wallington grunted and shifted in place. *Hey! Mind saving me, you jackasses?!*

"Hang tight, Wallington... shouldn't be too hard for you, I suppose."

The medic's next grunt displayed unmistakable frustration.

Ziler chuckled. "Hold on. Gotta use the flamethrower. Burning through that web will be the fastest way of getting you down." He turned to Graves and Browne. "Get back to the canoe. Float it down here. Guide it with some of the rope we found. Be super-freaking-careful.... but also act fast. If there are any other mosquitos flying around out there, I don't want to be here when they return home."

"You got it, Captain." Graves unpacked the flamethrower cannister, then ran with Browne to the canoes, 'accidentally' bumping into Liz as he went.

The angry virologist gave a scalding glance at the mercenaries. Her weapon was holstered, her hands now fumbling over that pack of Altoids.

Ziler knew what usually followed those mint candies. He chose to say nothing. There were more important things to worry about.

He picked up the nozzle and aimed it at the far-right side of the web. "I'll torch the ends and gradually work inward. Don't worry, Wallington. I'll be sure not to cook you."

CHAPTER 18

It traveled through the rainforest, using its keen sense of smell to guide itself to the precious nest. Its abdomen was swollen with loot taken from the body of a chimpanzee. Already, it had forgotten the event, its computer-like brain solely focused on the task at hand. The mosquito, and its twenty sisters who flew alongside it, were single-minded in their task of delivering blood to their nest.

Less than a day ago, they had lain their eggs. Since then, their primary goal was to hunt and bring back blood to nourish their brood. It was their only purpose in life. Their size rendered their original purpose in wildlife obsolete. Their normal-sized counterparts were pollinators, transferring pollen flower-to-flower as they fed on nectar. The size of their probiscis made such feedings difficult for the mutants. From the moment of birth, they sought blood, for themselves and for their nest.

As it neared the nest, the mosquito detected a faint chemical scent, similar to those emitted by fire. It wasn't enough to repel it or its sisters, but it was enough to make them cautious. A chemical scent, no matter what it was, indicated another lifeform had entered the area.

After closing within a few hundred yards, they detected carbon dioxide. Drawing closer to their nest, it was clear that something had entered the cove. Like a missile defense system, their brains activated with the goal of seeking out these intruders.

The mosquito detected two groups, one in the cove, the other in the woods. It would be a quick process to eject its current blood supply into the nest and proceed with the attack. It was a sentiment shared by its twenty sisters. Those whose abdomens were only partially filled had the advantage of attacking first. Though they lived in unison, their very existence was nonstop competition. After all, they killed not only to nourish their young, but to feed themselves.

Fueled by bloodlust, they advanced toward the battleground.

***

"Third charge is set," Graves said.

He was kneeling at the southern end of the cove, watching the eggs carefully as he watched the block of C4 balancing between two of them. Browne was over on the east end of the cove, placing a few charges along the shoreline.

In the cove's center was the canoe. On its middle seat was the crate of highly unstable dynamite. Steering it into the cove was a slow and tense process that took ten years off Graves' life. Nothing made him jump more than the sound of a submerged branch bumping against the wooden hull. Through good luck or divine intervention, the impact was not hard enough to trigger the nitroglycerin.

The eggs came in handy, holding the canoe square in the middle of the cove. There was no concern of it drifting too far one way or the other. All the mercs had to worry about were the eggs hatching before they were done. The other canoe was beached at the mouth of the cove. Once the job was done, they would work their way back to the hut and take possession of the other canoe. With evening setting in, they would probably be forced to take shelter in one of the huts for the night, then go for the rendezvous point at dawn.

As long as the mosquitos were dead, Graves didn't mind one bit. He placed a fourth charge at the southwestern edge of the cove. That was the last of his explosives. Thanks to the contents in that crate, they had more than enough to get the job done.

Browne stood up and started working his way toward Graves, giving a thumbs up to signal his charges were set.

"Perfect." He got on his radio. "Cap, everything's set over here. Just waiting on you slowpokes."

"Just a couple more minutes. Nearly had a forest fire over here. Trying to get this crap off Wallington. Hold position. We'll be done shortly."

"Copy that."

A gunshot made him jump. He turned around, seeing Browne aiming his pistol at the water. Twenty feet out were the exploded remains of a mosquito larva that had recently hatched.

"Little warning next time," Graves said. Browne glared at him. Graves shrugged and walked away. "Yeah-yeah-yeah, I know. Can't talk. Or, can barely talk, whichever it is."

Another gunshot made him jump. Graves faced the water again, seeing the remains of another mosquito larva splattering the nest.

"Everything alright over there?" Ziler asked through the radio.

"Got a few eggs hatching," Graves said. He watched as a few of the soft, rounded objects began to pulsate, the silhouettes inside shifting radically. "We're gonna need to blow this place real soon, Captain. Otherwise, we'll be catering for one very unpleasant baby shower."

"Copy that."

Ziler shifted his mic downward and knelt beside Wallington. Most of the cocoon had been burnt or cut away, freeing his arms and legs. He had regained partial mobility, but was still extremely stiff from the spider's venom.

"Sorry, bud. We gotta get a move-on. Unless you'd like to witness the miracle of birth out there in the cove?"

Wallington shook his head. "N-no, thanks. I'll pass."

Ziler and Susan put his arms around their shoulders and lifted him to his feet. The medic gasped, his stiff muscles fighting against him. He tried to take a step, but for the most part, was heavily reliant on his two helpers.

"Where's Dr. Moore?" Susan asked.

Ziler looked around. "Dr. Moore? You here?" He waited a few moments and got no answer. "Dr. Moore, you better show yourself. We're not waiting any longer."

"I'm here, I'm here," Liz repeated. She emerged from behind one of the trees, her right hand stuffed in her back pocket. There was a mild sluggishness to her movements. Her eyes were drooped, her balance slightly off.

Ziler wasn't close enough to see her pupils, but given the fact that she was literally hiding behind a tree, it was clear the idiot had taken a fairly large dose of her 'special treat'.

He had no desire to confront her on it. She could overdose, for all he cared, as long as she waited until they were back at the village.

For a split-second, he considered confiscating her pistol. It was bad enough that she was untrustworthy to begin with, but now he was dealing with a drugged-up, nutjob of a scientist who was hellbent on getting her thumb-drive and vials back from Susan. She had not said anything yet. Ziler figured she was waiting for them to clear the area first.

Or, she had something else in mind.

He heard another gunshot coming from the cove. Probably one of the guys putting down another hatchling.

Another gunshot followed. Then another, and another, quickly escalating into automatic fire.

"We've got company!"

As soon as Graves spoke, Ziler heard the buzzing wings. There were hostiles inside the forest coming straight at them. He shifted Wallington's weight onto Susan and took firing position with his M27.

Pinpointing the source of the sound, he pivoted to his right. There it was, five meters away and closing fast. Its legs were outstretched, its spear-shaped mouth ready to sink deep into his body.

He met the bug with a volley of bullets. His aim was slightly off, hitting the insect in the upper left thorax, severing one of its legs and damaging its wing. It descended to the ground in a spiral, resembling a helicopter seed falling in spring. Hitting the ground, the bug thrashed its remaining legs.

Ziler finished it off with a headshot, then turned around as Susan shouted his name. Coming at her and Wallington were two other mosquitos. Ziler fired another shot, striking one at the joint between its abdomen and thorax. The larger segment fell free, the rest of the bug suddenly ascending as the still-fluttering wings had less weight to carry. The strength soon left the mosquito, who plummeted to the ground.

Its companion had no intention of joining its fate. The mosquito, slightly larger than the others, dove at a forty-five-degree angle.

Ziler shifted his aim, his finger applying pressure to the trigger.

BANG!

He felt the projectile strike his shoulder. Stunned, physically and mentally, he stumbled backward for several steps before falling to the ground. He could feel his blood wetting his left shoulder and the projectile lodged somewhere in the muscle.

He had been shot.

Glancing northwest, he spotted Liz ducking behind a tree, her pistol in hand. Her scheme was obvious and simple; kill him and Susan, leave them and Wallington to die, reclaim her samples, then claim to the others that the mosquitos had gotten them. With all the chaos and gunfire, they wouldn't have been able to distinguish her pistol shots from the other shooting taking place.

I knew I shouldn't have let that bitch have her gun back.

He aimed his rifle in her direction, but was forced to redirect it at the mosquito. It landed on top of him, and without hesitation, successfully plunged its proboscis into his shoulder—the same shoulder that had been shot.

Ziler yelled out. Immediately, he felt a strange rushing sensation, as though his bloodstream had turned into a raging river, heading directly for the wound in his shoulder. Knowing he had seconds to act, he slammed his rifle against the mosquito's head and pushed with every ounce of strength his body could spare.

The mosquito leaned back, its mouth gradually exiting the wound.

Ziler pushed a little further. The rushing feeling stopped. The mosquito was not ready to give up. It slashed his torso with its front legs, its head trying desperately to ram its proboscis into its victim.

He heard Susan scream. There was a blur of motion, then suddenly, the mosquito was no longer on top of him.

He rolled to his right and saw the virologist and the bug wrestling on the ground. Susan's hands were pressed against its torso, keeping its mouth at bay. Her strength was quickly waning. The insect was not impacted by fear or adrenaline. It was a simple organism, not hindered by outside factors such as disgust or fright. It only retreated when it had no other choice.

Ziler rolled to his knees and took aim.

A sixth sense kicked in. He could feel himself in the middle of a set of iron sights. He could almost hear the drawing of a breath one took before pulling the trigger.

"C-Cap!" Wallington groaned. The medic was trying to alert him.

Ziler spun on his heel, and spotted Liz Moore taking aim at him again. This time, he was the one to fire a shot. A pink mist exploded from her right shoulder.

Liz yelled out, her shot flying high as she reeled backward.

Ziler turned around and sprinted at the bug, kicking it off of Susan. He aimed down and squeezed the trigger. To his amazement, the bug managed to flutter its wings and fly off, disappearing into the canopy. He continued shooting after it, hoping to neutralize the assailant before it could double-back.

Susan was quick to return to her feet. Shrieking, she brushed her body, still feeling the mosquito's legs all over her.

"You're all right, Doctor," he said. He looked up, hearing more buzzing wings in the canopy. "But we better get moving."

They ran over to Wallington and lifted him to his feet.

"What about Dr. Moore?" Susan asked.

Ziler glanced in Liz's direction. She was moaning in pain, grasping her wounded shoulder.

"Don't leave me here," she said.

Ziler's eyes went back to the trees. The big mother mosquito and two of her sisters were making a fast descent straight for the easy prey. Even if he wanted to, there was no hope of rescuing her.

"Damn it, Ziler! I'll double your price!" He shook his head. "I'm retired."

"Damn you, Ziler! Get me out of here—AHHHHH!"

Liz snatched her pistol out of the grass and, without aiming, frantically shot rounds at the trio of bugs. To Ziler's amazement, she actually managed to hit one, its limp body dropping directly on her from thirty feet. The impact cracked ribs and compressed her stomach, forcing its contents through her mouth.

The other two bugs landed on their victim. One sank its jaw into her thigh and began suctioning.

The larger mosquito mounted her chest, exposing its proboscis. Liz let out one final scream, which was quickly silenced as the spear-tipped jaw plunged into her mouth. She squirmed, her flesh hugging her bones as every drop of blood was suctioned out of her body.

With the bugs distracted, Ziler and Susan carried Wallington toward the cove, running as fast as their legs could carry them.

Every direction Graves turned, there were mosquitos flying about. In the open space above the cove, they flew all over the place, making it difficult to land a shot.

He popped off rounds, each missed shot feeling like a punch to the gut.

"Hold still, ya pricks!"

Browne managed to hit one, its battered corpse splashing down in the cove. The bugs swooped lower and lower, legs extended, zig-zagging in quick bursts of motion. Browne fired off a few rounds, missing. There were at least four bugs converging on him, kept at bay only by the startling muzzle flashes.

Several others gathered near Graves, darting in random directions, looking for an opening to attack.

"Shit! Shit! Shit! Shit!" He squeezed the trigger with each "shit", right up until he heard the *click* of an empty magazine. "SHIT!!!"

One of the bugs lunged, striking him from behind. Graves fell forward, cursing upon impact with the mud. He rolled onto his back, seeing the mosquito mounting his torso, ready to draw blood. He unholstered his pistol and shoved its muzzle into the mosquito's face.

"Buzz off!"

A squeeze of the trigger sent a bullet through the insect's brain. He kicked its fresh corpse off of him and tried to stand up, only to be driven to the ground again by another mosquito.

"Damn it! Damn it! Damn it!"

Bang! Bang! Bang!

All sense of tactical training disappeared. Spurred by overwhelming fright, Graves put several rounds into the mosquito, killing it. Once again, another mosquito quickly took its place. It dove from his right, its outstretched leg inadvertently slapping his wrist. Graves felt the pistol spiral out of his grip, rendering him unarmed.

The mosquito planted its razor-tipped legs on him, pinning him down. Its sibling joined in, the two bugs briefly fighting for space.

Sneering, Graves pushed the bugs off of him. In that moment, one of them drove its mouthpart forward with intent to stab his chest. The proboscis instead pierced his palm, its tip protruding out the other side.

Seeing his hand skewered on the bug's mouth, Graves writhed in agony. Despite the pain, he used the leverage to keep the bony tube away from his body.

It was a plan with limited benefit. The second mosquito bared its jaw, dripping green fluid onto his torso. Graves tensed. He kicked his legs but failed to shake the thing off.

There was nothing to do but accept the inevitable.

The bug positioned itself, pointed its jaw downward as though operating a jackhammer, then drove its jaw home.

The only impact was that of a nine-millimeter bullet striking its head.

Graves looked over his shoulder, seeing Browne racing toward him with his pistol outstretched. Behind him were several mosquitos, gradually closing in. Browne kept his focus on the bug atop of his brother-in-arms. He fired three times, his shots landing inches above Grave's impaled hand. The bug's head cracked open, its tiny brain turned to mush.

Browne turned around one-hundred-eighty degrees to take on the bugs that tracked him. He emptied the rest of the magazine into one of them. The other three closed in simultaneously, giving him no time to reload.

He tossed the weapon aside in favor of his knives. He held his karambit in one hand and a buck knife in the other. He remained perfectly still, allowing his six-legged opponents to close the distance.

Up close and personal, man and insect collided, slashing and stabbing. The lead bug met him head on, planting its forelegs on his shoulders. Its jaw came down behind his collarbone, instantaneously plunging three inches into his body. With the bug in a fixed position, Browne proceeded to stab with his knives. The bug convulsed as two blades cracked its shell and pierced internal organs. He twisted the knives, doing maximum damage before retracting the buck knife. With a powerful thrust, he put the blade in its head, ending its life before it could drain his.

The other two circled from behind, landing on their target as he killed their sibling. Two jaws plunged deep into his back, each one managing to find a lung. With the breath literally sucked out of him, Browne fell to his knees, his eyes wide. Not willing to accept defeat, he reached over his shoulder, seizing one of the bugs by its antennae. Growling, he pulled, extracting its mouth from its body and bringing its head in front of him.

Holding his buck knife in reverse grip, he stabbed like a slasher villain, putting multiple holes in the mosquito's head before it stopped thrashing.

In those moments, he felt his blood suctioning out through his back. The remaining mosquito gorged, its abdomen swelling and turning red. Browne dropped to his knees, the knives falling from his hands. The strength had left his body. In a few moments, his life would follow.

A gunshot echoed across the cove.

The bug's limp body fell off Browne, its head split open by a rifle shot. Browne and Graves looked to the forest as Ziler, Susan, and Wallington stepped out.

Susan held on to the medic while the Captain fired a few more shots in the air, successfully dropping another mosquito. He hurried beside Graves and reached into the side pocket of his pants.

"I could make a joke about what you're doing," Graves said.

"Shut up." Ziler pulled the two flare sticks from Graves' pocket, sparked a flame, and waved them high. Deterred by the chemical scent and the bright flare, the bugs increased their elevation. They hovered a hundred feet high, unwilling to allow their prey to escape.

Ziler helped Graves to pry his hand free of the dead mosquito's proboscis, then helped him to his feet.

"Can you stand?"

"Yeah. Won't be able to shoot straight though," Graves replied, pulling some gauze from another pocket and wrapping it around his hand. "Help Browne."

Susan was already by the knife-wielder's side. She looked to Ziler, shaking her head.

"The wounds are deep. His lungs are damaged, he's lost a lot of blood…"

With shaky hands, Browne pulled the detonator from his vest. He tilted his head toward the river, his final word coming out in a low growl.

"Go!" The rest of his statement was unspoken, but well-understood. *I'm not gonna make it. Let me go out with a bang.*

Graves fired a few rounds at the air. The fiery deterrent was starting to fail. Gradually, the bugs were ready to initiate another attack.

Ziler accepted the facts. Even if they got Browne out of here, it was unlikely he would survive the trip in this condition. He knew the former Army Ranger well enough to know he would rather go out in a literal blaze of glory than slowly die on a canoe.

He stood up, put his heels together, and offered his man a final salute. Browne returned the gesture.

Graves took his place, his injured hand tucked near his chest.

"Thanks for saving my ass. Sorry about all the jokes about your jaw."

Browne snorted, then picked up his buck knife, extending it to Graves. It was his favorite of all the blades he owned, having been in his possession since he was a kid. From hunting trips to combat missions, Browne carried it wherever he went. If ever there was a souvenir to remember him by, it was this blade.

"Thanks, bro."

Without saying anything more, the four of them ran for the river.

Browne eased himself on his back, keeping the detonator close to his body. The bugs danced high above him, unsure if they wanted to pursue the survivors, or go for the easy prey below.

Their hesitation granted him enough time to pick his pistol off the ground and reload it. Though he planned to die, he hoped to at least get one more of the bastards before blowing himself up. He scooted himself closer to the shore, right next to one of the C4 explosives.

Slamming a fresh mag into place, Browne took aim at the swarm. Unleashing all seventeen rounds, he took out one of their numbers.

The flares fizzled and died.

Like vultures descending on a dead critter, the mosquitos descended on him. Browne smiled. There was pleasure in knowing he had tricked the stupid bugs into flying straight into their doom.

Down they went, crowding his body, stabbing it.

None of them got to taste his blood. Browne's thumb pressed the button. The C4 discharged, triggering the dynamite.

In one millisecond, the cove was a hot mass of flame and smoldering bugs and eggs. Burning egg casings, wings, legs, and other body parts spat across the clearing, resembling meteor fragments. The downward shockwave rippled through the cove, imploding every single egg in the area.

***

In its two weeks of life, the mosquito had tasted the blood of over thirty victims. It was a simple process of attacking its victim and returning to its nest. Standard, routine, automatic. All blood was the same, as was its nutritional effect.

Until now.

It beat its wings, unsure if it wanted to fly or not. It lacked the cognitive ability to realize that the human corpse it had recently drained had blood that was contaminated with a narcotic. It felt lethargic, its body unaccustomed to the strange substance it had unknowingly ingested. Its companion was the same, remaining perched on the trunk of a nearby tree. Their brains, unable to develop a pleasure high, instead developed extreme aggression.

Adding to their newfound hostility was the sense of thirst they experienced. It came about suddenly, triggering a need to intake fresh blood. Like with their normal-sized counterparts, thirst resulted in heightened aggression.

Then came the shockwave from a tremendous explosion. Both bugs took to the sky and darted toward the cove. Immediately, they were repelled by the intense heat. They ascended and flew north, momentarily focused on self-preservation.

After gaining some distance, the two insects detected carbon dioxide being expelled from exhausted organisms near the river. Fueled by aggression, the two bugs pursued, the larger of the pair taking the lead. The fact that their abdomens were filled with blood meant nothing. They needed to feed.

To kill.

***

"Easy… easy…" Ziler said, carefully lowering Wallington into the canoe with Susan's help. The boat was in the water, waiting for its occupants to come aboard. "Easy…"

Graves looked to the woods, holding his pistol in his left hand. Beyond the crackling fire and falling debris behind them, he could hear something else. Something all too familiar.

"Captain? I think we've got incoming."

Ziler froze and listened. "Shit." He dropped Wallington into the canoe, who landed with a frustrated yelp.

"You said easy," the medic said.

"Shh!" Ziler pointed his muzzle at the forest.

"On your two o'clock," Graves said.

Two bugs, one larger than the other, tore from the canopy and nosedived straight for the humans. Both mercenaries opened fire.

Shifting its attention to the canoe, the larger mosquito zagged left, avoiding the volley of bullets. Its companion took a hit to its center mass, yet kept coming, for its brain failed to detect the injuries. It slammed right into Graves.

For the second time that evening, the mercenary was on his back fighting off a giant mosquito. Also, for the second time, he pushed its head away with his right hand, keeping its jaw at bay.

"I swear, every day from now on, whenever I leave the house, I'm bringing a giant can of bug spray everywhere I go."

He pressed his pistol to the mosquito's eye and squeezed the trigger, emptying his magazine into its brain.

Susan screamed, swinging the oar as the final mosquito hovered over her. Her motions rocked the canoe, causing it to drift several feet into the river. The mosquito followed it, bobbing up and down, looking for an opening in her defense.

Ziler approached the shore and elevated his muzzle, ready to blast the bug out of the air. Had he had just one more moment, he would have been successful. Alas, the mosquito found the opening it craved.

Susan swung the oar and missed, exposing her right side. The bug lunged, seizing her in its six legs. With nowhere else to go, Susan reeled backwards, taking the bug with her into the river.

Ziler lowered his muzzle and ran to the waterline. Wallington was in the canoe, struggling to pull himself up. On the other side, the scientist and insect tussled in the water.

With no way to shoot the bug without hitting Susan, the mercenary had no choice but to dive in.

"Hey, boss!" Graves shouted. He tossed Browne's buck knife to the Captain, who caught it by the handle. He unsheathed his own knife and proceeded into the water.

Susan lifted her head and took a breath. She submerged, the insect taking her place. While drowning in the river, it refused to abandon the opportunity to kill the human. Its uncomplicated brain had gone haywire. Only murder made sense.

Ziler threw himself on its back. The bug reared backward, knocking him backward. It turned around, using its wings as propellors as it pressed the attack. Ziler found himself pinned against the riverbed.

A yell of pain exploded with a slew of air bubbles. The mosquito punched its mouthpart into his thigh. The water was too dark and murky for him to see the oversized pest, but he could feel its weight on his legs.

Ziler sat up and slashed with Browne's knife. The blade hit something rigid, triggering a shuddering motion from the bug. He slashed again and again, hitting the same spot.

Crack!

The bug shifted its weight, freeing him. Ziler still felt the object in his thigh muscle, but no sense of his blood being drained. He stood up, bringing his head above water. The bug was several feet ahead of him, shaking its wings and legs. A green substance spewed from its head.

Sheathing his tactical knife, Ziler felt the puncture wound on his leg. He pulled the instrument out and held it in the evening sunlight. He had severed the bug's proboscis.

He reversed his grip, pointing the spear-like tip downward like a dagger. The insect continued flailing in the water, its main weapon now in the hands of its enemy.

Ziler lunged, the mouthpart raised high over his head. He brought it down hard, driving its own mouth through its eye, deep into its brain. Green blood and other translucent fluid spurted from the wound.

The bug convulsed, its limbs spasming as though hit with ten-thousand volts of electricity.

"Join your larvae... in hell." He twisted the proboscis. After a final jolt, the bug went limp. Ziler pushed its body to the side and walked over to Susan. She was standing upright, slowly catching her breath.

They stood together, watching the corpse drift downriver.

"Okay... I'm moving to Antarctica," she said. "No more bugs for me."

"As long as the next project doesn't involve mutant polar bears," Ziler replied. "Don't count on me saving your ass in that instance."

They shared a laugh and went to shore, pulling the canoe alongside them. Graves was sitting on the grass, tending to his injured hand.

"You alright there, Captain?" he said, pointing to Ziler's injured shoulder and leg.

"I'll be sore for a little while, but I'll live," Ziler said.

Graves looked to the sky. "It's getting dark. Do we want to take our chances on the canoe or lay low in the huts until dawn?"

Ziler grimaced. With the excitement now over, his injuries were starting to throb. He was no stranger to pain, but the thought of spending the night in the jungle where his wounds could get severely infected was not appealing. Less so than chancing the river in the dark.

"I don't know how we'll call the helicopter," Susan said. "I lost the SAT phone during the attack on the barge."

"Radio station at the landing point was intact," Ziler said. "We'll use that to radio the base."

"Fine with me," Susan said, taking a seat in the canoe. She helped Wallington sit upright. The medic winced, the venom slowly wearing off. "I for one am ready to get the hell out of here. I think your man here feels the same."

Graves stood up and went straight for the canoe. "You heard the lady."

"You giving orders now?" Ziler said.

"Job's over," Graves replied. "We're retired now."

Ziler smiled and stepped aboard, handing back Browne's buck knife. "Sounds good to me."

"Just one more thing left to do," Susan said. She pulled the thumb drive and vials from her pocket. Now more than ever, she was eager to expose Lexington to the world. "I assume you fellas have connections. You know any hard-hitting journalists with a stick up his ass that has nothing better to do than bring down a major company?"

Ziler chuckled. "I'm sure I know one or two." He winced, his injuries aching like hell. "First thing's first, let's get the hell out of here."

"Got no arguments from me," Graves said, slipping the knife into a vest pocket. He took the oar and plunged it into the water.

The long journey home began.

The End

Made in the USA
Las Vegas, NV
02 December 2023

81961742R00090